PENGUIN BOOKS

The Book of Sand *and* Shakespeare's Memory

'He more than anyone renovated the language of fiction and thus opened the way to a remarkable generation of Spanish-American novelists. Gabriel García Márquez, Carlos Fuentes, José Donoso, and Mario Vargas Llosa have all acknowledged a debt to him'
J. M. Coetzee, *New York Review of Books*

'Borges was the quintessential writer's writer . . . he proved himself to be one of the towering figures of literature in Spanish'
James Woodall, *Guardian*

'I love his work because every one of his pieces contains a model of the universe or an attribute of the universe . . . because his stories often take the outer form of some genre from popular literature, a form proved by long usage, which creates almost mythical structures' Italo Calvino

'What Borges offered his readers was a philosophy, an ethical system, a method . . . for the craft of following a revelatory thread through the labyrinth of the universe' Alberto Manguel, *Observer*

'He creates, outside time and space, imaginary and symbolic worlds. It is a sign of his importance that, in placing him, only strange and perfect works can be called to mind' André Maurois

'He is the seer who appears, as if in a dream, to lead the votary forward . . . In one essay he says of Joyce that "he is less a man of letters than a literature". We may without hesitation apply the same description to Borges himself, with the codicil that his is the literature of eternity'
Peter Ackroyd, *The Times*

Jorge Luis Borges was born in Buenos Aires in 1899 and educated in Europe. One of the most widely acclaimed writers of our time, he published many collections of poems, essays and short stories, before his death in Geneva in June 1986. In 1961 Borges shared the International Publishers' Prize with Samuel Beckett. The Ingram Merrill Foundation granted him its Annual Literary Award in 1966 for his 'outstanding contribution to literature'. In 1971 Columbia University awarded him the first of many degrees of Doctor of Letters, *honoris causa*, that he was to receive from the English-speaking world. In 1971 he received the fifth biennial Jerusalem Prize and in 1973 was given the Alfonso Reyes Prize, one of Mexico's most prestigious cultural awards. In 1980 he shared the Cervantes Prize (the Spanish world's highest literary accolade) with Gerardo Diego. Borges was Director of the Argentine National Library from 1955 until 1973. In a tribute to Borges, Mario Vargas Llosa wrote: 'His is a world of clear, pure, and at the same time unusual ideas . . . expressed in words of great directness and restraint. [He] was a superb storyteller. One reads most of Borges' tales with the hypnotic interest usually reserved for reading detective fiction . . .'

Several volumes of his work are published or forthcoming in Penguin.

Andrew Hurley is Professor of English at the University of Puerto Rico in San Juan, where he also teaches in the Translation Program. He has translated Reinaldo Arenas's *Pentagony* novels as well as works by Fernando Arrabal, Ernesto Sabato, Gustavo Sainz and, most recently, the Puerto Rican authors Edgardo Rodríguez Juliá, Ana Lydia Vega and Antonio Martorell.

JORGE LUIS BORGES

The Book of Sand and Shakespeare's Memory

Translated with an Afterword by Andrew Hurley

PENGUIN BOOKS

PENGUIN BOOKS

Published by the Penguin Group
Penguin Books Ltd, 27 Wrights Lane, London w8 5tz, England
Penguin Putnam Inc., 375 Hudson Street, New York, New York 10014, USA
Penguin Books Australia Ltd, Ringwood, Victoria, Australia
Penguin Books Canada Ltd, 10 Alcorn Avenue, Toronto, Ontario, Canada m4v 3b2
Penguin Books India (P) Ltd, 11, Community Centre, Panchsheel Park, New Delhi – 110 017, India
Penguin Books (NZ) Ltd, Private Bag 102902, NSMC, Auckland, New Zealand
Penguin Books (South Africa) (Pty) Ltd, 5 Watkins Street, Denver Ext 4, Johannesburg 2094, South Africa

Penguin Books Ltd, Registered Offices: Harmondsworth, Middlesex, England

These translations first published in *Collected Fictions*
in the USA by Viking Penguin, a member of Penguin Putnam Inc., 1998
First published in Great Britain by Allen Lane The Penguin Press 1999
Published in Penguin Books 2000
The Book of Sand and *Shakespeare's Memory* published as a
separate volume in Penguin Classics 2001
1

Set in 11/13.25 pt PostScript Monotype Columbus
Typeset by Rowland Phototypesetting Ltd, Bury St Edmunds, Suffolk
Printed in England by Clays Ltd, St Ives plc

Contents

The Book of Sand
(1975)

The Other

The incident occurred in February, 1969, in Cambridge, north of Boston. I didn't write about it then because my foremost objective at the time was to put it out of my mind, so as not to go insane. Now, in 1972, it strikes me that if I do write about what happened, people will read it as a story and in time I, too, may be able to see it as one.

I know that it was almost horrific while it lasted—and it grew worse yet through the sleepless nights that followed. That does not mean that anyone else will be stirred by my telling of it.

It was about ten o'clock in the morning. I was sitting comfortably on a bench beside the Charles River. Some five hundred yards to my right there was a tall building whose name I never learned. Large chunks of ice were floating down the gray current. Inevitably, the river made me think of time . . . Heraclitus' ancient image. I had slept well; the class I'd given the previous evening had, I think, managed to interest my students. There was not a soul in sight.

Suddenly, I had the sense (which psychologists tell us is associated with states of fatigue) that I had lived this moment before. Someone had sat down on the other end of my bench. I'd have preferred to be alone, but I didn't want to get up immediately for fear of seeming rude. The other man had started whistling. At that moment there occurred the first of the many shocks that morning was to bring me. What the man was whistling—or *trying* to whistle (I have never been able to carry a tune)—was the popular Argentine milonga *La tapera,* by Elías Regules. The tune carried me back to a patio that no longer exists and to the memory of Alvaro Melián Lafinur, who died so many years ago. Then there came the words. They were the words of the *décima* that begins the song. The voice was not Alvaro's but it tried to imitate Alvaro's. I recognized it with horror.

I turned to the man and spoke.

"Are you Uruguayan or Argentine?"

"Argentine, but I've been living in Geneva since '14," came the reply.

There was a long silence. Then I asked a second question.

"At number seventeen Malagnou, across the street from the Russian Orthodox Church?"

He nodded.

"In that case," I resolutely said to him, "your name is Jorge Luis Borges. I too am Jorge Luis Borges. We are in 1969, in the city of Cambridge."

"No," he answered in my own, slightly distant, voice, "I am here in Geneva, on a bench, a few steps from the Rhône."

Then, after a moment, he went on:

"It *is* odd that we look so much alike, but you are much older than I, and you have gray hair."

"I can prove to you that I speak the truth," I answered. "I'll tell you things that a stranger couldn't know. In our house there's a silver *mate* cup with a base of serpents that our great-grandfather brought from Peru. There's also a silver washbasin that was hung from the saddle. In the wardrobe closet in your room, there are two rows of books: the three volumes of Lane's translation of the *Thousand and One Nights*—which Lane called *The Arabian Nights Entertainment*—with steel engravings and notes in fine print between the chapters, Quicherat's Latin dictionary, Tacitus' *Germania* in Latin and in Gordon's English version, a *Quixote* in the Garnier edition, a copy of Rivera Indarte's *Tablas de sangre*

4

signed by the author, Carlyle's *Sartor Resartus*, a biography of Amiel, and, hidden behind the others, a paperbound volume detailing the sexual customs of the Balkans. Nor have I forgotten a certain afternoon in a second-floor apartment on the Plaza Dubourg."

"Dufour," he corrected me.

"All right, Dufour," I said. "Is that enough for you?"

"No," he replied. "Those 'proofs' of yours prove nothing. If I'm dreaming you, it's only natural that you would know what I know. That longwinded catalog of yours is perfectly unavailing."

His objection was a fair one.

"If this morning and this encounter are dreams," I replied, "then each of us does have to think that he alone is the dreamer. Perhaps our dream will end, perhaps it won't. Meanwhile, our clear obligation is to accept the dream, as we have accepted the universe and our having been brought into it and the fact that we see with our eyes and that we breathe."

"But what if the dream should last?" he asked anxiously.

In order to calm him—and calm myself, as well—I feigned a self-assurance I was far from truly feeling.

"My dream," I told him, "has already lasted for seventy years. And besides—when one wakes up, the person one meets is always oneself. That is what's happening to us now, except that we are two. Wouldn't you like to know something about my past, which is now the future that awaits you?"

He nodded wordlessly. I went on, a bit hesitatingly:

"Mother is well, living happily in her house in Buenos Aires, on the corner of Charcas and Maipú, but Father died some thirty years ago. It was his heart. He had had a stroke—that was what finally killed him. When he laid his left hand over his right, it was like a child's hand resting atop a giant's. He died impatient for death, but without a word of complaint. Our grandmother had died in the same house. Several days before the end, she called us all in and told us, 'I am an old, old woman, dying very slowly. I won't have anyone making a fuss over such a common, ordinary thing as that.' Norah, your sister, is married and has two children. By the way—at home, how is everyone?"

"Fine. Father still always making his jokes against religion. Last night he said Jesus was like the gauchos, who'll never commit themselves, which is why He spoke in parables."

He thought for a moment, and then asked: "What about you?"

"I'm not sure exactly how many books you'll write, but I know there are too many. You'll write poetry that will give you a pleasure that others will not fully share, and stories of a fantastic turn. You will be a teacher—like your father, and like so many others of our blood."

I was glad he didn't ask me about the success or failure of the books. I then changed my tack.

"As for history . . . There was another war, with virtually the same antagonists. France soon capitulated; England and America battled a German dictator named Hitler—the cyclical Battle of Waterloo. Buenos Aires engendered another Rosas in 1946, much like our kinsman, the first one.* In '55, the province of Córdoba saved us, as Entre Ríos had before. Things are bad now. Russia is taking over the planet; America, hobbled by the superstition of democracy, can't make up its mind to be an empire. Our own country is more provincial with every passing day—more provincial and more self-important, as though it had shut its eyes. I shouldn't be surprised if the teaching of Latin were replaced by the teaching of Guaraní."

I realized that he was barely listening. The elemental fear of the impossible yet true had come over him, and he was daunted. I, who have never been a father, felt a wave of love for that poor young man who was dearer to me than a child of my own flesh and blood. I saw that his hands were clutching a book. I asked what he was reading.

6

"*The Possessed*—or, as I think would be better, *The Devils*, by Fyodor Dostoievsky," he answered without vanity.

"It's a bit hazy to me now. Is it any good?"

The words were hardly out of my mouth when I sensed that the question was blasphemous.

"The great Russian writer," he affirmed sententiously, "has penetrated more deeply than any other man into the labyrinths of the Slavic soul."

I took that rhetorical pronouncement as evidence that he had grown calmer.

I asked him what other works by Dostoievsky he had read.

He ticked off two or three, among them *The Double*.

I asked him whether he could tell the difference between the characters when he read, as one could with Joseph Conrad, and whether he planned to read on through Dostoievsky's entire corpus.

"The truth is, I don't," he answered with a slight note of surprise.

I asked him what he himself was writing, and he told me he was working on a book of poetry to be called *Red Anthems*. He'd also thought about calling it *Red Rhythms* or *Red Songs*.

"Why not?" I said. "You can cite good authority for it—Rubén Darío's blue poetry and Verlaine's gray song."

Ignoring this, he clarified what he'd meant—his book would be a hymn to the brotherhood of all mankind. The modern poet cannot turn his back on his age.

I thought about this for a while, and then asked if he really felt that he was brother to every living person—every undertaker, for example? every letter carrier? every undersea diver, everybody that lives on the even-numbered side of the street, all the people with laryngitis? (The list could go on.) He said his book would address the great oppressed and outcast masses.

"Your oppressed and outcast masses," I replied, "are nothing but an abstraction. Only individuals exist—if, in fact, anyone

7

Yesterday's man is not today's, as some Greek said. We two, on this bench in Geneva or in Cambridge, are perhaps the proof of that."

Except in the austere pages of history, memorable events go unaccompanied by memorable phrases. A man about to die tries to recall a print that he glimpsed in his childhood; soldiers about to go into battle talk about the mud or their sergeant. Our situation was unique and, frankly, we were unprepared. We talked, inevitably, about literature; I fear I said no more than I customarily say to journalists. My *alter ego* believed in the imagination, in creation—in the discovery of new metaphors; I myself believed in those that correspond to close and widely acknowledged likenesses, those our imagination has already accepted: old age and death, dreams and life, the flow of time and water. I informed the young man of this opinion, which he himself was to express in a book, years later.

But he was barely listening. Then suddenly he spoke.

"If you have been me, how can you explain the fact that you've forgotten that you once encountered an elderly gentleman who in 1918 told you that he, too, was Borges?"

I hadn't thought of that difficulty. I answered with conviction.

"Perhaps the incident was so odd that I made an effort to forget it."

He ventured a timid question.

"How's your memory?"

I realized that for a mere boy not yet twenty, a man of seventy-some-odd years was practically a corpse.

"It's often much like forgetfulness," I answered, "but it can still find what it's sent to find. I'm studying Anglo-Saxon, and I'm not at the foot of the class."

By this time our conversation had lasted too long to be a conversation in a dream.

I was struck by a sudden idea.

"I can prove to you this minute," I said, "that you aren't

8

dreaming me. Listen to this line of poetry. So far as I can recall, you've never heard it before."

I slowly intoned the famous line: "*L'hydre-univers tordant son corps écaillé d'astres.*"

I could sense his almost fear-stricken bafflement. He repeated the line softly, savoring each glowing word.

"It's true," he stammered, "I could never write a line like that."

Hugo had brought us together.

I now recall that shortly before this, he had fervently recited that short poem in which Whitman recalls a night shared beside the sea—a night when Whitman had been truly happy.

"If Whitman sang of that night," I observed, "it's because he desired it but it never happened. The poem gains in greatness if we sense that it is the expression of a desire, a longing, rather than the narration of an event."

He stared at me.

"You don't know him," he exclaimed. "Whitman is incapable of falsehood."*

A half century does not pass without leaving its mark. Beneath our conversation, the conversation of two men of miscellaneous readings and diverse tastes, I realized that we would not find common ground. We were too different, yet too alike. We could not deceive one another, and that makes conversation hard. Each of us was almost a caricature of the other. The situation was too unnatural to last much longer. There was no point in giving advice, no point in arguing, because the young man's inevitable fate was to be the man that I am now.

Suddenly I recalled a fantasy by Coleridge. A man dreams that he is in paradise, and he is given a flower as proof. When he wakes up, there is the flower.

I hit upon an analogous stratagem.

"Listen," I said, "do you have any money?"

"Yes," he replied. "About twenty francs. I invited Simón Jichlinski to have dinner with me at the Crocodile tonight."

"Tell Simón that he'll practice medicine in Carouge, and that he will do a great deal of good . . . now, give me one of your coins."

He took three silver pieces and several smaller coins out of his pocket. He held out one of the silver pieces to me; he didn't understand.

I handed him one of those ill-advised American bills that are all of the same size though of very different denominations. He examined it avidly.

"Impossible!" he cried. "It's dated 1964."

(Months later someone told me that banknotes are not dated.)

"This, all this, is a miracle," he managed to say. "And the miraculous inspires fear. Those who witnessed the resurrection of Lazarus must have been terrified."

We haven't changed a bit, I thought. Always referring back to books.

He tore the bill to shreds and put the coin back in his pocket.

I had wanted to throw the coin he gave me in the river. The arc of the silver coin disappearing into the silver river would have lent my story a vivid image, but fate would not have it.

I replied that the supernatural, if it happens twice, is no longer terrifying; I suggested that we meet again the next day, on that same bench that existed in two times and two places.

He immediately agreed, then said, without looking at his watch, that it was getting late, he had to be going. Both of us were lying, and each of us knew that the other one was lying. I told him that someone was coming to fetch me.

"Fetch you?" he queried.

"Yes. When you reach my age, you'll have almost totally lost your eyesight. You'll be able to see the color yellow, and light and shadow. But don't worry. Gradual blindness is not tragic. It's like the slowly growing darkness of a summer evening."

We parted without having touched one another. The next day, I did not go to the bench. The other man probably didn't, either.

I have thought a great deal about this encounter, which I've never told anyone about. I believe I have discovered the key to it. The encounter was real, but the other man spoke to me in a dream, which was why he could forget me; I spoke to him while I was awake, and so I am still tormented by the memory.

The other man dreamed me, but did not dream me *rigorously*— he dreamed, I now realize, the impossible date on that dollar bill.

Ulrikke ✓

Hann tekr sverthit Gram ok leggr i methal theira bert
Völsunga Saga, 27

My story will be faithful to reality, or at least to my personal recollection of reality, which is the same thing. The events took place only a short while ago, but I know that the habit of literature is also the habit of interpolating circumstantial details and accentuating certain emphases. I wish to tell the story of my encounter with Ulrikke (I never learned her last name, and perhaps never will) in the city of York. The tale will span one night and one morning.

It would be easy for me to say that I saw her for the first time beside the Five Sisters at York Minster, those stained glass panes devoid of figural representation that Cromwell's iconoclasts left untouched, but the fact is that we met in the dayroom of the Northern Inn, which lies outside the walls. There were but a few of us in the room, and she had her back to me. Someone offered her a glass of sherry and she refused it.

"I am a feminist," she said. "I have no desire to imitate men. I find their tobacco and their alcohol repulsive."

The pronouncement was an attempt at wit, and I sensed this wasn't the first time she'd voiced it. I later learned that it was not like her—but what we say is not always like us.

She said she'd arrived at the museum late, but that they'd let her in when they learned she was Norwegian.

"Not the first time the Norwegians storm York," someone remarked.

"Quite right," she said. "England was ours and we lost her—if, that is, anyone can possess anything or anything can really be lost."

It was at that point that I looked at her. A line somewhere in William Blake talks about girls of soft silver or furious gold, but in Ulrikke there was both gold and softness. She was light and tall, with sharp features and gray eyes. Less than by her face, I was impressed by her air of calm mystery. She smiled easily, and her smile seemed to take her somewhere far away. She was dressed in black—unusual in the lands of the north, which try to cheer the dullness of the surroundings with bright colors. She spoke a neat, precise English, slightly stressing the *r*'s. I am no great observer; I discovered these things gradually.

We were introduced. I told her I was a professor at the University of the Andes, in Bogotá. I clarified that I myself was Colombian.

"What is 'being Colombian'?"

"I'm not sure," I replied. "It's an act of faith."

"Like being Norwegian," she said, nodding.

I can recall nothing further of what was said that night. The next day I came down to the dining room early. I saw through the windows that it had snowed; the moors ran on seamlessly into the morning. There was no one else in the dining room. Ulrikke invited me to share her table. She told me she liked to go out walking alone.

I remembered an old quip of Schopenhauer's.

"I do too. We can go out alone together," I said.

We walked off away from the house through the newly fallen snow. There was not a soul abroad in the fields. I suggested we go downriver a few miles, to Thorgate. I know I was in love with Ulrikke; there was no other person on earth I'd have wanted beside me.

Suddenly I heard the far-off howl of a wolf. I have never heard a wolf howl, but I know that it was a wolf. Ulrikke's expression did not change.

After a while she said, as though thinking out loud:

"The few shabby swords I saw yesterday in York Minster were more moving to me than the great ships in the museum at Oslo."

Our two paths were briefly crossing: that evening Ulrikke was to continue her journey toward London; I, toward Edinburgh.

"On Oxford Street," she said, "I will retrace the steps of de Quincey, who went seeking his lost Anna among the crowds of London."

"De Quincey," I replied, "stopped looking. My search for her, on the other hand, continues, through all time."

"Perhaps," Ulrikke said softly, "you have found her."

I realized that an unforeseen event was not to be forbidden me, and I kissed her lips and her eyes. She pushed me away with gentle firmness, but then said:

"I shall be yours in the inn at Thorgate. I ask you, meanwhile, not to touch me. It's best that way."

For a celibate, middle-aged man, proffered love is a gift that one no longer hopes for; a miracle has the right to impose conditions. I recalled my salad days in Popayán and a girl from Texas, as bright and slender as Ulrikke, who had denied me her love.

I did not make the mistake of asking her whether she loved me. I realized that I was not the first, and would not be the last. That adventure, perhaps the last for me, would be one of many for that glowing, determined disciple of Ibsen.

We walked on, hand in hand.

"All this is like a dream," I said, "and I never dream."

"Like that king," Ulrikke replied, "who never dreamed until a sorcerer put him to sleep in a pigsty."

Then she added:

"Ssh! A bird is about to sing."

In a moment we heard the birdsong.

"In these lands," I said, "people think that a person who's soon to die can see the future."

"And I'm about to die," she said.

I looked at her, stunned.

"Let's cut through the woods," I urged her. "We'll get to Thorgate sooner."

"The woods are dangerous," she replied.

We continued across the moors.

"I wish this moment would last forever," I murmured.

"*Forever* is a word mankind is forbidden to speak," Ulrikke declared emphatically, and then, to soften her words, she asked me to tell her my name again, which she hadn't heard very well.

"Javier Otárola," I said.

She tried to repeat it, but couldn't. I failed, likewise, with *Ulrikke*.

"I will call you Sigurd," she said with a smile.

"And if I'm to be Sigurd," I replied, "then you shall be Brunhild."

Her steps had slowed.

"Do you know the saga?" I asked.

"Of course," she said. "The tragic story that the Germans spoiled with their parvenu Nibelungen."

I didn't want to argue, so I answered:

"Brunhild, you are walking as though you wanted a sword to lie between us in our bed."

We were suddenly before the inn. I was not surprised to find that it, like the one we had departed from, was called the Northern Inn.

From the top of the staircase, Ulrikke called down to me:

"Did you hear the wolf? There are no wolves in England anymore. Hurry up."

As I climbed the stairs, I noticed that the walls were papered a deep crimson, in the style of William Morris, with intertwined birds and fruit. Ulrikke entered the room first. The dark chamber

15

had a low, peaked ceiling. The expected bed was duplicated in a vague glass, and its burnished mahogany reminded me of the mirror of the Scriptures. Ulrikke had already undressed. She called me by my true name, Javier. I sensed that the snow was coming down harder. Now there was no more furniture, no more mirrors. There was no sword between us. Like sand, time sifted away. Ancient in the dimness flowed love, and for the first and last time, I possessed the image of Ulrikke.

The Congress ✓

Ils s'acheminèrent vers un château immense, au frontis-
pice duquel on lisait: "Je n'appartiens à personne et
j'appartiens à tout le monde. Vous y étiez avant que
d'y entrer, et vous y serez encore quand vous en
sortirez."   Diderot: *Jacques Le Fataliste et son Maître* (1769)

My name is Alexander Ferri. There are martial echoes in the name,
but neither the trumpets of glory nor the great shadow of the
Macedonian (the phrase is borrowed from the author of *Los
mármoles*, whose friendship I am honored to claim) accord very
well with the gray, modest man who weaves these lines on the
top floor of a hotel on Calle Santiago del Estero in a Southside
that's no longer the Southside it once was. Any day now will
mark the anniversary of my birth more than seventy years ago; I
am still giving English lessons to very small classes of students.
Indecisiveness or oversight, or perhaps other reasons, led to my
never marrying, and now I am alone. I do not mind solitude;
after all, it is hard enough to live with oneself and one's own
peculiarities. I can tell that I am growing old; one unequivocal
sign is the fact that I find novelty neither interesting nor surprising,
perhaps because I see nothing essentially new in it—it's little
more than timid variations on what's already been. When I was
young, I was drawn to sunsets, slums, and misfortune; now it is
to mornings in the heart of the city and tranquility. I no longer
play at being Hamlet. I have joined the Conservative Party and

a chess club, which I attend as a spectator—sometimes an absentminded one. The curious reader may exhume, from some obscure shelf in the National Library on Calle México, a copy of my book *A Brief Examination of the Analytical Language of John Wilkins*, a work which ought to be republished if only to correct or mitigate its many errors. The new director of the library, I am told, is a literary gentleman who has devoted himself to the study of antique languages, as though the languages of today were not sufficiently primitive, and to the demagogical glorification of an imaginary Buenos Aires of knife fighters. I have never wished to meet him. I arrived in this city in 1899, and fate has brought me face to face with a knife fighter, or an individual with a reputation as one, exactly once. Later, if the occasion presents itself, I will relate that incident.

I have said that I am alone; a few days ago, a fellow resident here in the hotel, having heard me talk about Fermín Eguren, told me that he had recently died, in Punta del Este.

I find my sadness over the death of that man (who most emphatically was never my friend) to be curiously stubborn. I know that I am alone; I am the world's only custodian of the memory of that *geste* that was the Congress, a memory I shall never share again. I am now its only delegate. It is true that all mankind are delegates, that there is not a soul on the planet who is not a delegate, yet I am a member of the Congress in another way—I *know* I am; that is what makes me different from all my innumerable colleagues, present and future. It is true that on February 7, 1904, we swore by all that's sacred—is there anything on earth that is sacred, or anything that's not?—that we would never reveal the story of the Congress, but it is no less true that the fact that I am now a perjurer is also part of the Congress. That statement is unclear, but it may serve to pique my eventual readers' curiosity.

At any rate, the task I have set myself is not an easy one. I have never attempted to produce narrative prose, even in its epistolary form; to make matters worse, no doubt, the story I am about to tell is not believable. It was the pen of José Fernández Irala, the undeservedly forgotten poet of *Los mármoles*, that fate had destined for this enterprise, but now it is too late. I will not deliberately misrepresent the facts, but I can foresee that sloth and clumsiness will more than once lead me into error.

The exact dates are of no importance. I would remind the reader that I came here from Santa Fe, the province of my birth, in 1899. I have never gone back; I have grown accustomed to Buenos Aires (a city I am not, however, particularly fond of) like a person grown accustomed to his own body, or an old ache. I sense, though I find little interest in the fact, that my death is near; I should, therefore, hold in check my tendency to digress, and get on with telling the story.

Years do not change our essence, if in fact we have an essence; the impulse that led me one night to the Congress of the World was that same impulse that had initially betaken me to the city room of the newspaper *Ultima Hora.** For a poor young man from the provinces, being a newspaperman can be a romantic life, much as a poor young man from the big city might conceive a gaucho's life to be romantic, or the life of a peon on his little piece of land. I am not embarrassed to have wanted to be a journalist, a profession which now strikes me as trivial. I recall having heard my colleague Fernández Irala say that the journalist writes to be forgotten, while he himself wanted to write to be remembered, and to last. By then he had already sculpted (the word was in common use) some of the perfect sonnets that were to appear sometime later, with the occasional slight retouching, in the pages of *Los mármoles*.

I cannot put my finger on the first time I heard someone mention the Congress. It may have been that evening when the paymaster paid me my monthly salary and to celebrate that proof that I was now a part of Buenos Aires I invited Irala to have dinner with me. Irala said he was sorry, he couldn't that night, he couldn't miss the Congress. I immediately realized that he was not referring to that pompous, dome-capped building at the far end of an avenue on which so many Spaniards chose to live, but rather to something more secret, and more important. People talked about the Congress—some with open contempt, others with lowered voices, still others with alarm or curiosity; all, I believe, in ignorance. A few Saturdays later, Irala invited me to go with him. He had seen, he said, to all the necessary arrangements.

It was somewhere between nine and ten at night. On the trolley, Irala told me that the preliminary meetings took place on Saturday and that don Alejandro Glencoe, perhaps inspired by my name, had already given leave for me to attend. We went into the Confitería del Gas.* The delegates, some fifteen or twenty I would say, were sitting around a long table; I am not certain whether there was a raised dais or whether memory has added it. I recognized the chairman immediately, though I had never seen him before. Don Alejandro was a gentleman of dignified air, well past middle age, with a wide, frank forehead, gray eyes, and a red beard flecked generously with white. I never saw him in anything but a dark frock coat; he tended to sit with his crossed hands resting on his walking stick. He was tall, and robust-looking. To his left sat a much younger man, likewise with red hair; the violent color of this latter fellow's hair suggested fire, however, while the color of Glencoe's beard was more like autumn leaves. To Glencoe's right sat a young man with a long face and a singularly low forehead, and quite the dandy. Everyone had ordered coffee; one and another had also ordered absinthe. The first thing that caught my attention was the presence of a woman, the only one among so many men. At the other end of the table there was a boy about ten years old, dressed in a sailor suit; he soon fell asleep. There were also a Protestant minister, two unequivocal Jews, and a Negro with a silk kerchief and very tight clothing in the style street corner toughs affected in those days. Before the Negro and the boy there sat cups of chocolate. I cannot recall the others, except for one Sr. Marcelo del Mazo, a man of exquisite manners and cultured conversation, whom I never saw again. I still have a blurred and unsatisfactory photograph of one of the meetings, though I shan't publish it because the clothing of the period, the hair and mustaches, would leave a comical and even seedy impression that would misrepresent the scene. All organizations tend to create their own dialects and their own rituals; the Congress, which was always slightly dreamlike to me, apparently wanted its delegates to discover gradually, and without haste, the goal that the Congress sought, and even the Christian names and patronymics of their colleagues. I soon realized that I was under an obligation not to ask questions, and so I abstained from questioning Fernández Irala, who for his own part volunteered nothing. I missed not a single Saturday, but a month or two passed before I understood. From the second meeting on, the person who sat next to me was Donald Wren, an engineer for the Southern Railway, who would later give me English lessons.

Don Alejandro spoke very little; the others did not address him directly, but I sensed that they were speaking for his benefit and sought his approval. A wave of his slow hand sufficed to change the subject of discussion. Little by little I discovered that the red-haired man to his left bore the odd name Twirl. I recall the impression of frailty he gave—the characteristic of certain very tall men, as though their height gave them vertigo and made them stoop. His hands, I recall, often toyed with a copper compass, which from time to time he would set on the table. He died in late 1914, an infantryman in an Irish regiment. The man who always sat at don Alejandro's right was the beetle-browed young man, Fermín Eguren, the chairman's nephew. I am not a believer in the methods of realism, an artificial genre if ever there was one; I prefer to reveal from the very beginning, and once and for all, what I only gradually came to know. But before that, I want to remind the reader of my situation at that time: I was a poor young man from Casilda, the son of farmers; I had made my way to Buenos Aires and suddenly found myself, or so I felt, at the very center of that great city—perhaps, who can say, at the center of the world. A half century has passed, yet I still feel that first sense of dazzled bewilderment—which would by no means be the last.

These, then, are the facts; I will relate them very briefly:

Don Alejandro Glencoe, the chairman, was a rancher from the eastern province,* the owner of a country estate on the border with Brazil. His father, originally from Aberdeen, had settled in South America in the middle of the last century. He had brought with him some hundred or so books—the only books, I daresay, that don Alejandro had ever read in his life. (I mention these heterogeneous books, which I have held in my own hands, because one of them contained the seed from which my tale springs.) When the elder Glencoe died, he left a daughter and a son; the son would grow up to be our chairman. The daughter, who married a man named Eguren, was Fermín's mother. Don Alejandro ran once for the House of Deputies, but political bosses barred his way to the Uruguayan Congress. This rebuff rankled him, and he resolved to found *another* Congress—a Congress of enormously grander scope. He recalled having read in one of Carlyle's volcanic pages of the fate of that Anacharsis Cloots, worshiper of the goddess Reason, who stood at the head of thirty-six foreigners and spoke, as the "spokesman for the human race," before an assembly in Paris. Inspired by Cloots' example, don Alejandro conceived the idea of establishing a Congress of the World, which would represent all people of all nations. The headquarters for the organizational meetings was the Confitería del Gas; the opening ceremonies, set for four years thence, would take place at don Alejandro's ranch. He, like so many Uruguayans, was no follower of Artigas,* and he loved Buenos Aires, but he was determined that the Congress should meet in his homeland. Curiously, the original date for that first meeting would be met with almost magical exactness.

At first we received a not inconsiderable honorarium for the meetings we attended, but the zeal that inflamed us all caused Fernández Irala, who was as poor as I was, to renounce his, and we others all followed suit. That gesture turned out to be quite salutary, as it separated the wheat from the chaff; the number of delegates dropped, and only the faithful remained. The only salaried position was that of the secretary, Nora Erfjord, who had no other means of subsistence and whose work was overwhelming. Keeping tabs on an entity which embraced the entire planet was no trivial occupation. Letters flew back and forth, as did telegrams. Messages of support came in from Peru, Denmark, and Hindustan. A Bolivian gentleman pointed out that his country was totally landlocked, with no access to the sea whatsoever, and suggested that that deplorable condition should be the topic of one of our first debates.

Twirl, a man of lucid intelligence, remarked that the Congress presented a problem of a philosophical nature. Designing a body of men and women which would represent all humanity was akin to fixing the exact number of Platonic archetypes, an enigma that has engaged the perplexity of philosophers for centuries. He suggested, therefore, that (to take but one example) don Alejandro Glencoe might represent ranchers, but also Uruguayans, as well as founding fathers and red-bearded men and men sitting in armchairs. Nora Erfjord was Norwegian. Would she represent secretaries, Norwegians, or simply all beautiful women? Was one engineer sufficient to represent all engineers, even engineers from New Zealand?

It was at that point, I believe, that Fermín interrupted.

"Ferri can represent wops,"* he said with a snort of laughter.

Don Alejandro looked at him sternly.

"Sr. Ferri," don Alejandro said serenely, "represents immigrants, whose labors are even now helping to build the nation."

Fermín Eguren could never stand me. He thought highly of himself on several counts: for being a Uruguayan, for coming of native stock, for having the ability to attract women, for having discovered an expensive tailor, and, though I shall never know why, for being descended from the Basques—a people who, living always on the margins of history, have never done anything but milk cows.

One particularly trivial incident sealed our mutual enmity. After one of our sessions, Eguren suggested that we go off to Calle Junín.* The idea held little interest for me, but I agreed, so as not to expose myself to his raillery. Fernández Irala went with us. As we were leaving the house we had been to, we bumped into a big, burly brute of a man. Eguren, who'd no doubt been drinking a little too much, gave him a shove. The other man blocked our way angrily.

"The man that wants to leave here is going to have to get past this knife," he said.

I remember the gleam of the blade in the dimness of the vestibule. Eguren stepped back, terrified. I was scared, too, but my anger got the better of my fear. I put my hand inside my jacket, as though to pull out a knife.

"Let's settle this in the street," I said in a steady voice.

The stranger answered back, his voice changed.

"That's a man to my own heart! I just wanted to test you fellows, friend."

Now he was chuckling.

"*You* used the word 'friend,' I didn't," I rejoined, and we walked out.

The man with the knife went on into the whorehouse. I was told later that his name was Tapia or Paredes or something of the sort, and that he was a famous troublemaker. Out on the sidewalk, Irala, who'd been calm up to that point, slapped me on the back.

"At least there was one musketeer among the three of us!" he exclaimed. "*Salve, d'Artagnan!*"

Fermín Eguren never forgave me for having witnessed him back down.

I feel that it is at this point, and only at this point, that the story begins. The pages that have gone before have recorded only the conditions required by chance or fate in order for the incredible event (perhaps the only event of my entire life) to occur. Don Alejandro Glencoe was always at the center of the web of plans, but we gradually began to feel, not without some astonishment and alarm, that the real chairman was Twirl. This singular individual with his flaming mustache fawned upon Glencoe and even Fermín Eguren, but with such exaggeration that the fawning might be taken for mockery, and therefore not compromise his dignity. Glencoe prided himself upon his vast fortune, and Twirl figured out that all it took to saddle Glencoe with some new project was to suggest that the undertaking might be too costly. At first, I suspect, the Congress had been little more than a vague name; Twirl was constantly proposing ways to expand it, and don Alejandro always went along. It was like being at the center of an ever-widening, endlessly expanding circle that seemed to be moving farther and farther beyond one's reach. Twirl declared, for example, that the Congress could not do without a library of reference books; Nierenstein, who worked in a bookstore, began bringing us the atlases of Justus Perthes and sundry encyclopedias, from Pliny's *Historia Naturalis* and Beauvais' *Speculum* to the pleasant labyrinths (I reread these pages with the voice of Fernández Irala) of the illustrious French *encyclopédistes*, of the *Britannica*, of Pierre Larousse, Brockhaus, Larsen, and Montaner y Simón. I recall having reverently caressed the silky volumes of a certain Chinese encyclopedia, the beautiful brush-strokes of its characters seeming more mysterious to me than the spots on a leopard's skin. I will not reveal at this point the fate those silken pages met, a fate I do not lament.

Don Alejandro had conceived a liking for Fernández Irala and me, perhaps because we were the only delegates that did not try to flatter him. He invited us to spend a few days with him on his ranch, La Caledonia, where the carpenters, chosen from among the laborers on the estate, were already hard at work.

After a long journey upriver and a final crossing on a raft, we stepped one morning onto the eastern shore. Even after all that, we had to pass several nights in poverty-stricken general stores and open and close many a gate in many a stock fence across the Cuchilla Negra. We were riding in a gig; the landscape seemed much larger and more lonely to me than that of the little plot where I was born.

I still retain my two distinct images of the ranch: the one I'd pictured to myself before we arrived and the one my eyes actually took in. Absurdly, I had imagined, as though in a dream, an impossible combination of the flatlands around Santa Fe and the Palace of Running Waters*: La Caledonia was in fact a long adobe house with a peaked roof of thatched straw and a brick gallery. To my eyes, it looked built to last: the rough walls were almost a yard thick, and the doors were narrow. No one had thought of planting a tree; the place was battered by the first sun of morning and the last sun of evening. The corrals were of stone; the herd was large, the cows skinny and behorned; the swirling tails of the horses reached the ground. I tasted for the first time the meat of a just-slaughtered animal. The men brought out sacks of hardtack; a few days later, the foreman told me he'd never tasted bread in his life. Irala asked where the bathroom was; don Alejandro swept his arm through the air expansively, as much as to say "the entire continent." It was a moonlit night; I went out for a walk and came upon him, watched over by a rhea.

The heat, which nightfall had not softened, was unbearable, but everyone exclaimed over the evening's coolness. The rooms were low-ceiling'd and numerous, and they seemed run-down to me; Irala and I were given one that faced south. It had two cots and a washstand, whose pitcher and basin were of silver. The floor was of packed earth.

The next day I came upon the library and its volumes of Carlyle, and I looked up the pages devoted to that spokesman for the human race, Anacharsis Cloots, who had brought me to that morning and that solitude. After breakfast (identical to dinner) don Alejandro showed us the site of the Congress' new headquarters. We rode out a league on horseback, across the open plains. Irala, who sat his horse more than a bit nervously, had a spill.

"That city boy really knows how to get off a horse," the foreman said with a straight face.

We saw the building from a distance. A score or so of men had raised a sort of amphitheater, still in bits and pieces. I recall scaffolding, and tiers of seats through which one could glimpse stretches of sky.

More than once I tried to converse with the gauchos, but every attempt failed. Somehow they knew they were different. But they were sparing with their words even among themselves, speaking their nasal, Brazilianized sort of Spanish. No doubt their veins carried Indian and Negro blood. They were strong, short men; in La Caledonia I was tall, which I had never been before. Almost all of them wore the *chiripá*, and some wore the wide-legged *bombacha*.* They had little or nothing in common with the mournful characters in Hernández or Rafael Obligado.* Under the spur of their Saturday alcohol, they could be casually violent. There were no women, and I never heard a guitar.

But the men that lived on that frontier did not make as great an impression on me as the complete change that had taken place in don Alejandro. In Buenos Aires he was an affable, moderate man; in La Caledonia, he was the stern patriarch of a clan, as his forebears had been. Sunday mornings he would read the Scripture to the laborers on his ranch; they understood not a word. One night, the foreman, a youngish man who had inherited the position from his father, came to tell us that a sharecropper and one of the laborers were about to have a knife fight. Don Alejandro stood up unhurriedly. He went out to the ring of men, took off the weapon he always wore, gave it to the foreman (who seemed to have turned fainthearted at all this), and stepped between the two blades. Immediately I heard his order:

"Put those knives down, boys."

Then in the same calm voice he added:

"Now shake hands and behave yourselves. I'll have no squawks of this sort here."

The two men obeyed. The next day I learned that don Alejandro had dismissed the foreman.

I felt I was being imprisoned by the solitude. I feared I would never make it back to Buenos Aires. I can't say whether Fernández Irala shared that fear, but we talked a great deal about Argentina and what we would do when we got back. I missed not the places one ordinarily might miss but rather the lions at the entrance to a house on Calle Jujuy near the Plaza del Once,* or the light from a certain store of inexact location. I was always a good rider; I soon fell into the habit of mounting a horse and riding for great distances. I still remember that big piebald I would saddle up— surely he's dead by now. I might even have ridden into Brazil one afternoon or evening, because the frontier was nothing but a line traced out by boundary stones.

I had finally taught myself not to count the days when, after a day much like all the others, don Alejandro surprised us.

"We're turning in now," he informed us. "Tomorrow morning we'll be leaving at first light."

Once I was downriver I began to feel so happy that I could actually think about La Caledonia with some affection.

We began to hold our Saturday sessions again. At the first meeting, Twirl asked for the floor. He said (with his usual flowery turn of phrase) that the library of the Congress of the World must not be limited to reference books alone—the classics of every land and language were a treasure we overlooked, he declared, only at our peril. His motion was passed immediately; Fernández Irala and Dr. Cruz, a professor of Latin, undertook to choose the necessary texts. Twirl had already spoken with Nierenstein about the matter.

At that time there was not an Argentine alive whose Utopia

was not Paris. Of us all, the man who champed at the bit the most was perhaps Fermín Eguren; next was Fernández Irala, for quite different reasons. For the poet of *Los mármoles*, Paris was Verlaine and Leconte de Lisle; for Eguren, an improved extension of Calle Junín. He had come to an understanding, I presume, with Twirl. At another meeting, Twirl brought up the language that would be used by the delegates to the Congress, and he suggested that two delegates be sent immediately to London and Paris to do research. Feigning impartiality, he first proposed my name; then, after a slight pause, the name of his friend Eguren. Don Alejandro, as always, went along.

I believe I mentioned that Wren, in exchange for a few lessons in Italian, had initiated me into the study of that infinite language English. He passed over grammar and those manufactured "classroom" sentences (insofar as possible) and we plunged straight into poetry, whose forms demand brevity. My first contact with the language that would fill my life was Stevenson's courageous "Requiem"; after that came the ballads that Percy unveiled to the decorous eighteenth century. A short while before my departure for London, I was introduced to the dazzling verse of Swinburne, which led me (though it felt like sin) to doubt the preeminence of Irala's alexandrines.

I arrived in London in early January of 1902. I recall the caress of the snow, which I had never seen before, and which I must say I liked. Happily, I had not had to travel with Eguren. I stayed at a modest inn behind the British Museum, to whose library I would repair morning and afternoon, in search of a language worthy of the Congress of the World. I did not neglect the universal languages; I looked into Esperanto (which Lugones' *Lunario sentimental**** calls "reasonable, simple, and economical") and Volapük, which attempts to explore all the possibilities of language, declining verbs and conjugating nouns. I weighed the arguments for and against reviving Latin (for which one still finds some nostalgia, even after so many centuries). I also devoted some

time to a study of the analytical language of John Wilkins, in
which the definition of each word is contained in the letters that
constitute it. It was under the high dome of the reading room that
I met Beatrice.

This is the general history of the Congress of the World, not
the history of Alexander Ferri—emphatically not my own—and
yet the first includes the second, as it includes all others. Beatrice
was tall and slender, her features pure and her hair bright red; it
might have reminded me of the devious Twirl's, but it never did.
She was not yet twenty. She had left one of the northern counties
to come and study literature at the university. Her origins, like
mine, were humble. In the Buenos Aires of that time, being of
Italian extraction was a questionable social recommendation; in
London I discovered that for many people it was romantic. It took
us but a few afternoons to become lovers; I asked her to marry
me, but Beatrice Frost, like Nora Erfjord, was a votary of the
religion of Ibsen and would not join herself to any man. From
her lips came the word I dared not speak. Oh nights, oh shared
warm darkness, oh love that flows in shadow like a secret river,
oh that moment of joy in which two are one, oh innocence and
openness of delight, oh the union into which we entered, only to
lose ourselves afterward in sleep, oh the first soft lights of day,
and myself contemplating her.

On that harsh border with Brazil I had been prey to homesick-
ness; not so in the red maze of London, which gave me so many
things. But in spite of the pretexts I invented to put off my
departure, at the end of the year I had to return; we would
celebrate Christmas together. I promised her that don Alejandro
would ask her to join the Congress; she replied, vaguely, that
she'd like to visit the Southern Hemisphere—a cousin of hers,
she said, a dentist, had settled in Tasmania. Beatrice had no wish
to see the boat off; farewells, in her view, were an emphasis, a
senseless celebration of misfortune, and she hated emphases. We
parted at the library where we had met the previous winter. I am

a coward; to avoid the anguish of waiting for her letters, I did not give her my address.

I have noticed that return voyages are shorter than voyages out, but that particular crossing of the Atlantic, wallowing in memories and heavy seas, seemed inordinately long to me. Nothing pained me so much as thinking that Beatrice's life, parallel with my own, was continuing onward, minute by minute and night by night. I wrote a letter many pages long, and tore it up when we anchored in Montevideo. I arrived in my own country on a Thursday; Irala was at the dock to greet me. I returned to my old lodgings in Calle Chile. That day and the next we spent talking and walking; I wanted to recapture Buenos Aires. It was a relief to know that Fermín Eguren was still in Paris; the fact that I'd returned before him might somehow mitigate my long absence.

Irala was discouraged. Fermín was spending vast sums of money in Europe and more than once had disobeyed instructions to return immediately. That was all predictable enough. It was other news that I found more disturbing: despite the objections of Irala and Cruz, Twirl had invoked Pliny the Younger—who had affirmed that there was no book so bad that it didn't contain some good—to suggest that the Congress indiscriminately purchase collections of *La Prensa*, thirty-four hundred copies (in various formats) of *Don Quijote*, Balmes' *Letters*, and random collections of university dissertations, short stories, bulletins, and theater programs. "All things are testaments," he had said. Nierenstein had seconded him; don Alejandro, "after three thunderous Saturdays," had agreed to the motion. Nora Erfjord had resigned her post as secretary; she was replaced by a new member, Karlinski, who was a tool of Twirl's. The enormous packages now began piling up, uncataloged and without card files, in the back rooms and wine cellar of don Alejandro's mansion. In early July, Irala had spent a week in La Caledonia. The carpenters were not working. The foreman, questioned about this, explained that don

Alejandro had ordered the work halted, and the workers were feeling the time on their hands.

In London I had drafted a report (which need not concern us here); on Friday, I went to pay my respects to don Alejandro and deliver the manuscript to him. Fernández Irala went with me. It was that hour of the evening when the pampas wind begins to blow; the house was filled with breezes. Before the iron gate on Calle Alsina there stood a wagon with three horses. I recall men, bent under the weight of their loads, carrying large bundles into the rear patio; Twirl was imperiously ordering them about. There too, as though they'd had a foreboding, were Nora Erfjord and Nierenstein and Cruz and Donald Wren and one or two others. Nora put her arms around me and kissed me, and that embrace, that kiss, reminded me of others. The Negro, high-spirited and gay, kissed my hand.

In one of the bedrooms the square trap-door to the cellar was lying open; crude cement steps led down into the dimness.

Suddenly we heard footsteps. Even before I saw him, I knew it was don Alejandro arriving home. He was almost running when he came into the room.

His voice was changed. It was not the voice of the thoughtful, deliberate gentleman who presided over our Saturday meetings, nor was it the voice of the feudal seigneur who stopped a knife fight and read the word of God to his gauchos, though it did resemble this latter one. He did not look at anyone when he spoke.

"Start bringing up everything that's piled down there," he commanded. "I don't want a book left in that cellar."

The job took almost an hour. In the earthen-floored patio we made a pile of books taller than the tallest among us. We all worked, going back and forth until every book had been brought up; the only person that did not move was don Alejandro.

Then came the next order:

"Now set that mound afire."

Twirl was pallid. Nierenstein managed to murmur:

"The Congress of the World cannot do without these precious aids that I have chosen with such love."

"The Congress of the World?" said don Alejandro, laughing scornfully—and I had never heard him laugh.

There is a mysterious pleasure in destruction; the flames crackled brightly while we cowered against the walls or huddled into the bedrooms. Night, ashes, and the smell of burning lingered in the patio. I recall a few lost pages that were saved, lying white upon the packed earth. Nora Erfjord, who professed for don Alejandro that sort of love that young women sometimes harbor for old men, finally, uncomprehending, spoke:

"Don Alejandro knows what he's doing."

Irala, one of literature's faithful, essayed a phrase:

"Every few centuries the Library at Alexandria must be burned."

It was then that we were given the explanation for all this.

"It has taken me four years to grasp what I am about to tell you. The task we have undertaken is so vast that it embraces— as I now recognize—the entire world. It is not a handful of prattling men and women muddying issues in the barracks of some remote cattle ranch. The Congress of the World began the instant the world itself began, and it will go on when we are dust. There is no place it is not. The Congress is the books we have burned. It is the Caledonians who defeated the Cæsars' legions. It is Job on the dunghill and Christ on the Cross. The Congress is even that worthless young man who is squandering my fortune on whores."

I could not restrain myself, and I interrupted.

"Don Alejandro, I am guilty too. I had finished my report, which I have here with me, but I stayed on in England, squandering your money, for the love of a woman."

"I supposed as much, Ferri," he said, and then continued: "The Congress is my bulls. It is the bulls I have sold and the leagues of countryside that do not belong to me."

An anguished voice was raised; it was Twirl's.

"You're not telling us you've sold La Caledonia?"

Don Alejandro answered serenely:

"I have. Not an inch of land remains of what was mine, but my ruin cannot be said to pain me because now I understand. We may never see each other again, because we no longer need the Congress, but this last night we shall all go out to contemplate the Congress."

He was drunk with victory; his firmness and his faith washed over us. No one thought, even for a second, that he had gone insane.

In the square we took an open carriage. I climbed into the coachman's seat, beside the coachman.

"Maestro," ordered don Alejandro, "we wish to tour the city. Take us where you will."

The Negro, standing on a footboard and clinging to the coach, never ceased smiling. I will never know whether he understood anything of what was happening.

Words are symbols that posit a shared memory. The memory I wish to set down for posterity now is mine alone; those who shared it have all died. Mystics invoke a rose, a kiss, a bird that is all birds, a sun that is the sun and yet all stars, a goatskin filled with wine, a garden, or the sexual act. None of these metaphors will serve for that long night of celebration that took us, exhausted but happy, to the very verge of day. We hardly spoke, while the wheels and horseshoes clattered over the paving stones. Just before dawn, near a dark and humble stream—perhaps the Maldonado, or perhaps the Riachuelo—Nora Erfjord's high soprano sang out the ballad of Sir Patrick Spens, and don Alejandro's bass joined in for a verse or two—out of tune. The English words did not bring back to me the image of Beatrice. Twirl, behind me, murmured:

"I have tried to do evil yet I have done good."

Something of what we glimpsed that night remains—the

reddish wall of the Recoleta, the yellow wall of the prison, two men on a street corner dancing the tango the way the tango was danced in the old days, a checkerboard entryway and a wrought-iron fence, the railings of the railroad station, my house, a market, the damp and unfathomable night—but none of these fleeting things (which may well have been others) matters. What matters is having felt that that institution of ours, which more than once we had made jests about, truly and secretly existed, and that it was the universe and ourselves. With no great hope, through all these years I have sought the savor of that night; once in a great while I have thought I caught a snatch of it in a song, in lovemaking, in uncertain memory, but it has never fully come back to me save once, one early morning, in a dream. By the time we'd sworn we would tell none of this to anyone, it was Saturday morning.

I never saw any of those people again, with the exception of Irala, and he and I never spoke about our adventure; any word would have been a profanation. In 1914, don Alejandro Glencoe died and was buried in Montevideo. Irala had died the year before.

I bumped into Nierenstein once on Calle Lima, but we pretended we didn't see each other.

There Are More Things

To the memory of H. P. Lovecraft

Just as I was about to take my last examination at the University of Texas, in Austin, I learned that my uncle Edwin Arnett had died of an aneurysm on the remote frontier of South America. I felt what we always feel when someone dies—the sad awareness, now futile, of how little it would have cost us to have been more loving. One forgets that one is a dead man conversing with dead men. The subject I was studying was philosophy; I recalled that there in the Red House near Lomas, my uncle, without employing a single proper noun, had revealed to me the lovely perplexities of the discipline. One of the dessert oranges was the tool he employed for initiating me into Berkeleyan idealism; he used the chessboard to explain the Eleatic paradoxes. Years later, he lent me Hinton's treatises, which attempt to prove the reality of a fourth dimension in space, a dimension the reader is encouraged to intuit by means of complicated exercises with colored cubes. I shall never forget the prisms and pyramids we erected on the floor of his study.

My uncle was an engineer. Before retiring from his job at the railway, he made the decision to move to Turdera,* which offered him the combined advantages of a virtual wilderness of solitude and the proximity of Buenos Aires. There was nothing more natural than that the architect of his home there should be his close friend Alexander Muir. This strict man professed the strict doctrine of Knox; my uncle, in the manner of almost all the gentlemen of his time, was a freethinker—or an agnostic, rather—yet at the same time he was interested in theology, the way he was interested in Hinton's fallacious cubes and the well-thought-out nightmares of the young Wells. He liked dogs; he had a big sheepdog he called Samuel Johnson, in memory of Lichfield, the distant town he had been born in.

The Red House stood on a hill, hemmed in to the west by swampy land. The Norfolk pines along the outside of the fence could not temper its air of oppressiveness. Instead of flat roofs where one might take the air on a sultry night, the house had a peaked roof of slate tiles and a square tower with a clock; these structures seemed to weigh down the walls and stingy windows of the house. As a boy, I accepted those facts of ugliness as one accepts all those incompatible things that only by reason of their coexistence are called "the universe."

I returned to my native country in 1921. To stave off lawsuits, the house had been auctioned off; it had been bought by a foreigner, a man named Max Preetorius, who paid double the amount bid by the next highest bidder. After the bill of sale was signed, he arrived one evening with two assistants and they threw all the furniture, all the books, and all the household goods in the house into a dump not far from the Military Highway. (I recall with sadness the diagrams in the volumes of Hinton and the great terraqueous globe.) The next day, he went to Muir and suggested certain changes to the house, which Muir indignantly refused to carry out. Subsequently, a firm from Buenos Aires undertook the work. The carpenters from the village refused to refurnish the house; a certain Mariani, from Glew,* at last accepted the conditions that Preetorius laid down. For a fortnight, he was to work at night, behind closed doors. And it was by night that the new resident of the Red House took up his habitation. The windows were never opened anymore, but through the darkness one could make out cracks of light. One morning the milkman came upon the body of the sheepdog, decapitated and mutilated, on the walk. That winter the Norfolk pines were cut down. No one ever saw Preetorius again; he apparently left the country soon after.

Such reports, as the reader may imagine, disturbed me. I know that I am notorious for my curiosity, which has, variously, led me into marriage with a woman utterly unlike myself (solely so that I might discover who she was and what she was really like), into trying laudanum (with no appreciable result), into an exploration of transfinite numbers, and into the terrifying adventure whose story I am about to tell. Inevitably, I decided to look into this matter.

My first step was to go and see Alexander Muir. I remembered him as a ramrod-straight, dark man whose leanness did not rule out strength; now he was stooped with years and his jet black beard was gray. He greeted me at the door of his house in Temperley—which predictably enough resembled my uncle's, as both houses conformed to the solid rules of the good poet and bad builder William Morris.

Our conversation was flinty; not for nothing is the thistle the symbol of Scotland. I sensed, however, that the strong Ceylon tea and the judicious plate of scones (which my host broke and buttered as though I were still a child) were, in fact, a frugal Calvinistic feast laid out to welcome his old friend's nephew. His theological debates with my uncle had been a long game of chess, which demanded of each player the collaborative spirit of an opponent.

Time passed and I could not bring myself to broach my subject. There was an uncomfortable silence, and then Muir himself spoke.

"Young man," he said, "you have not taken such trouble to come here to talk to me about Edwin or the United States, a country that holds little interest for me. What keeps you from sleeping at night is the sale of the Red House, and that curious individual that's bought it. Well, it keeps me from sleeping, too. Frankly, I find the whole affair most disagreeable, but I'll tell you what I can. It shan't be much."

In a moment, he went on, without haste.

"Before Edwin died, the mayor called me into his office. The parish priest was there. They wanted me to draw up the plans for a Catholic chapel. They would pay me well. I gave them my answer on the spot. No, I told them, I am a servant of the Lord, and I cannot commit the abomination of erecting altars for the worship of idols."

Here he stopped.

"That's all?" I hazarded.

"No. That Jewish whelp Preetorius wanted me to destroy my work, the house I'd built, and put up a monstrosity in its place. Abomination takes many forms."

He pronounced these words with great gravity, then he stood up.

As I turned the corner, Daniel Iberra approached me. We knew each other the way people in small towns do. He suggested we walk back together. I've never held any brief for hellions and that lot, and I could foresee a sordid string of more or less violent and more or less apocryphal bar stories, but I resigned myself and said I'd walk with him. It was almost dark. When he saw the Red House up on its hill a few blocks away, Iberra turned down another street. I asked him why. His answer was not what I'd expected.

"I'm don Felipe's right arm. Nobody's ever been able to say I backed down from anything. You probably remember that fellow Urgoiti that came all the way here from Merlo looking for me, and what happened to him when he found me. Well, listen—a few nights ago I was coming back from a big whoop-de-doo. About a hundred yards from the house, I saw something. My pinto spooked, and if I hadn't talked her down and turned down along that alleyway there, I might not be telling the story. What I saw was . . ." He shook his head. Then, angrily, he cursed.

That night I couldn't sleep. Toward sunrise I dreamed of an engraving in the style of Piranesi, one I'd never seen before or

39

Society defining the Mulatto as the Minotaur + Putting him in a labyrinth

perhaps had seen and forgotten—an engraving of a kind of labyrinth. It was a stone amphitheater with a border of cypresses, but its walls stood taller than the tops of the trees. There were no doors or windows, but it was pierced by an infinite series of narrow vertical slits. I was using a magnifying glass to try to find the Minotaur. At last I saw it. It was the monster of a monster; it looked less like a bull than like a buffalo, and its human body was lying on the ground. It seemed to be asleep, and dreaming— but dreaming of what, or of whom?

That evening I passed by the Red House. The gate in the fence was locked, and some iron bars had been twisted around it. What had been the garden was now weeds. Off to the right there was a shallow ditch, and its banks were trampled.

I had one card still up my sleeve, but I put off playing it for several days, not only because I sensed how utterly useless it would be but also because it would drag me to the inevitable, the ultimate.

Finally, with no great hopes, I went to Glew. Mariani, the carpenter, now getting on in years, was a fat, rosy Italian—a very friendly, unpretentious fellow. The minute I saw him I discarded the stratagems that had seemed so promising the day before. I gave him my card, which he spelled out to himself aloud with some ceremony, and with a slight reverential hitch when he came to the *Ph.D.* I told him I was interested in the furnishings he had made for the house that had belonged to my uncle, in Turdera. The man talked on and on. I will not attempt to transcribe his many (and expressively gesticulated) words, but he assured me that his motto was "meet the client's demands, no matter how outrageous," and told me he'd lived up to it. After rummaging around in several boxes, he showed me some papers I couldn't read, signed by the elusive Preetorius. (No doubt he took me for a lawyer.) When we were saying our good-byes, he confided that all the money in the world couldn't persuade him to set foot again in Turdera, much less in that house. He added that the customer is always right, but that in his humble opinion, Sr. Preetorius was "not *quite* right," if I knew what he meant—he tapped his forehead with his finger. Then, regretting he'd gone so far, he would say no more. I could get not another word out of him.

I had foreseen this failure, but it is one thing to foresee something, and another thing when it comes to pass.

Over and over I told myself that time—that infinite web of yesterday, today, the future, forever, never—is the only true enigma. Such profound thoughts availed me nothing; after dedicating my evening to the study of Schopenhauer or Royce I would still wander, night after night, along the dirt roads bordering the Red House. At times I would make out a very white light up on the hill; at others I would think I could hear moaning. This went on until the nineteenth of January.

It was one of those days in Buenos Aires when one feels not only insulted and abused by the summer, but actually degraded. It was about eleven that night when the storm clouds burst. First came the south wind, and then sheets, waves, torrents of water. I scurried about in the darkness, trying to find a tree to take shelter under. In the sudden sharp light from a bolt of lightning, I found that I was but steps from the fence. I am not certain whether it was with fear or hopefulness that I tried the gate. Unexpectedly, it opened. Buffeted by the storm, I made my way in; sky and earth alike impelled me. The front door of the house was also ajar. A gust of rain lashed my face, and I went in.

Inside, the floor tiles had been taken up; my feet trod grass in clumps and patches. A sweetish, nauseating odor filled the house. To the left or right, I am not sure which, I stumbled onto a stone ramp. I scrambled up it. Almost unthinkingly my hand sought the light switch.

The dining room and library of my recollections were now (the dividing wall having been torn out) one large ruinous room, with pieces of furniture scattered here and there. I will not attempt to describe them, because in spite of the pitiless white light I am

41

not certain I actually saw them. Let me explain: In order truly to see a thing, one must first understand it. An armchair implies the human body, its joints and members; scissors, the act of cutting. What can be told from a lamp, or an automobile? The savage cannot really perceive the missionary's Bible; the passenger does not see the same ship's rigging as the crew. If we truly saw the universe, perhaps we would understand it.

None of the insensate forms I saw that night corresponded to the human figure or any conceivable use. They inspired horror and revulsion. In one corner I discovered a vertical ladder that rose to the floor above. The wide iron rungs, no more than ten in all, were spaced irregularly; that ladder, which implied hands and feet, was comprehensible, and somehow it relieved me. I turned off the light and waited for a while in the darkness. I could hear not the slightest sound, but the presence of so many incomprehensible things unnerved me. At last, I made my decision.

Upstairs, my trembling hand once again reached out for the light switch. The nightmare prefigured by the downstairs rooms stirred and flowered in the upper story. There were many objects, or several interwoven ones. I now recall a long, U-shaped piece of furniture like an operating table, very high, with circular openings at the extremes. It occurred to me that this might be the bed used by the resident of the house, whose monstrous anatomy was revealed obliquely by this object in much the way the anatomy of an animal, or a god, may be known by the shadow it casts. From some page of Lucan, read years ago and then forgotten, there came to my lips the word *amphisbæna*, which suggested (though by no means fully captured) what my eyes would later see. I also recall a V of mirrors that faded into shadows above.

What must the inhabitant of this house be like? What must it be seeking here, on this planet, which must have been no less horrible to it than it to us? From what secret regions of astronomy or time, from what ancient and now incalculable twilight, had it reached this South American suburb and this precise night?

I felt that I had intruded, uninvited, into chaos. Outside, the rain had stopped. I looked at my watch and saw with astonishment that it was almost two A.M. I left the light on and began cautiously to climb back down the ladder. Climbing down what I had once climbed up was not impossible—climbing down before the inhabitant came back. I conjectured that it hadn't locked the front door and the gate because it hadn't known how.

My feet were just touching the next to last rung when I heard something coming up the ramp—something heavy and slow and plural. Curiosity got the better of fear, and I did not close my eyes.

The Sect of the Thirty

The original manuscript may be consulted in the library at the University of Leyden; it is in Latin, but its occasional Hellenism justifies the conjecture that it may be a translation from the Greek. According to Leisegang, it dates from the fourth century of the Christian era; Gibbon mentions it, in passing, in one of his notes to the fifteenth chapter of *The Decline and Fall*. These are the words of its anonymous author:

. . . The Sect was never large, but now its followers are few indeed. Their number decimated by sword and fire, they sleep by the side of the road or in the ruins spared them by war, as they are forbidden to build dwellings. They often go about naked. The events my pen describes are known to all men; my purpose here is to leave a record of that which has been given me to discover about their doctrine and their habits. I have engaged in long counsel with their masters, but I have not been able to convert them to Faith in Our Lord.

The first thing which drew my attention was the diversity of their opinion with respect to the dead. The most unschooled among them believe that they shall be buried by the spirits of those who have left this life; others, who do not cleave so tight to the letter, say that Jesus' admonition *Let the dead bury the dead* condemns the showy vanity of our funerary rites.

The counsel to sell all that one owns and give it to the poor is strictly observed by all; the first recipients give what they receive

44

to others, and these to yet others. This is sufficient explanation for their poverty and their nakedness, which likewise brings them closer to the paradisal state. Fervently they cite the words *Consider the ravens: for they neither sow nor reap: which neither have storehouse nor barn: and God feedeth them: how much more are ye better than the fowls?* The text forbids saving, for *If God so clothe the grass, which is today in the field, and tomorrow is cast into the oven: how much more will he clothe you, O ye of little faith? And seek not what ye shall eat, or what ye shall drink, neither be ye of doubtful mind.*

The prescription *Whosoever looketh on a woman to lust after her hath committed adultery with her already in his heart* is an unmistakable exhortation to purity. Still, many are the members of the Sect who teach that because there is no man under heaven who has not looked upon a woman to desire her, then we have all committed adultery. And since the desire is no less sinful than the act, the just may deliver themselves up without risk of hellfire to the exercise of the most unbridled lustfulness.

The Sect shuns churches; its teachers preach in the open, from a mountaintop or the top of a wall, or sometimes from a boat upturned upon the shore.

There has been persistent speculation as to the origins of the Sect's name. One such conjecture would have it that the name gives us the number to which the body of the faithful has been reduced; this is ludicrous but prophetic, as the perverse doctrine of the Sect does indeed predestine it to extinction. Another conjecture derives the name from the height of the Ark, which was thirty cubits; another, misrepresenting astronomy, claims that the name is taken from the number of nights within the lunar month; yet another, from the baptism of the Savior; another, from the age of Adam when he rose from the red dust. All are equally false. No less untruthful is the catalog of thirty divinities or *thrones,* of which, one is Abraxxas, pictured with the head of a cock, the arms and torso of a man, and the coiled tail of a serpent.

I know the Truth but I cannot plead the Truth. To me the

priceless gift of giving word to it has not been granted. Let others, happier men than I, save the members of the Sect by the word. By word or by fire. It is better to be killed than to kill oneself. I shall, therefore, limit myself to an account of the abominable heresy.

The Word was made flesh so that He might be a man among men, so that men might bind Him to the Cross, and be redeemed by Him. He was born from the womb of a woman of the chosen people not simply that He might teach the gospel of Love but also that He might undergo that martyrdom.

It was needful that all be unforgettable. The death of a man by sword or hemlock was not sufficient to leave a wound on the imagination of mankind until the end of days. The Lord disposed that the events should inspire pathos. That is the explanation for the Last Supper, for Jesus' words foretelling His deliverance up to the Romans, for the repeated sign to one of His disciples, for the blessing of the bread and wine, for Peter's oaths, for the solitary vigil on Gethsemane, for the twelve men's sleep, for the Son's human plea, for the sweat that was like blood, for the swords, the betraying kiss, the Pilate who washed his hands of it, the flagellation, the jeers and derision, the thorns, the purple and the staff of cane, the vinegar with honey, the Tree upon the summit of the Hill, the promise to the good thief, the earth that shook, and the darkness that fell upon the land.

Divine mercy, to which I myself owe so many blessings, has allowed me to discover the true and secret reason for the Sect's name. In Kerioth, where it is plausibly reputed to have arisen, there has survived a conventicle known as the Thirty Pieces of Silver. That was the Sect's original name, and it provides us with the key. In the tragedy of the Cross (and I write this with all the reverence which is its due) there were those who acted knowingly and those who acted unknowingly; all were essential, all inevitable. Unknowing were the priests who delivered the pieces of silver; unknowing, too, was the mob that chose Barabbas;

unknowing the Judean judge, the Romans who erected the Cross on which He was martyred and who drove the nails and cast the lots. Of knowing actors, there were but two: Judas and the Redeemer. Judas cast away the thirty coins that were the price of our souls' salvation and immediately hanged himself. At that moment he was thirty-three years old, the age of the Son of Man. The Sect venerates the two equally, and absolves the others.

There is not one lone guilty man; there is no man that does not carry out, wittingly or not, the plan traced by the All-Wise. All mankind now shares in Glory.

My hand fails when I will it to write a further abomination. The initiates of the Sect, upon reaching a certain age, are mocked and crucified on the peak of a mountain, to follow the example of their masters. This criminal violation of the Fifth Commandment should be met with the severity that human and divine laws have ever demanded. May the curses of the Firmament, may the hatred of angels . . .

The end of the manuscript has not been discovered.

The Night of the Gifts

It was in the old Café Aguila, on Calle Florida near the intersection of Piedad,* that we heard the story.

We were debating the problem of knowledge. Someone invoked the Platonic idea that we have already seen all things in some former world, so that "knowing" is in fact "recognizing"; my father, I think it was, said that Bacon had written that if learning was remembering, then not knowing a thing was in fact having forgotten it. Another member of the group, an elderly gentleman, who was no doubt a bit lost in all that metaphysics, decided to put in his two cents' worth. He spoke with slow assurance.

I've never been able to understand that business about Platonic archetypes. Nobody remembers the first time they saw yellow or black, or the first time they tasted some fruit—most likely because they were little and had no way of knowing they were at the beginning of a long, long series. There are other first times, of course, that nobody forgets. I could tell you fellows the memory of a certain night I often cast my mind back to—April 30, of '74.

Summers were longer in the old days, but I don't know why we'd stayed till such a late date at the place that some cousins of ours owned a few leagues from Lobos—Dorna, their name was. That was the summer that one of the laborers, a fellow named Rufino, initiated me into the customs of the country life. I was about to turn thirteen; he was a good bit older, and he had a reputation for being hot-tempered. He was quite a hand with a knife; when they practiced with burned sticks, the one that invariably wound up with a black smear across his face was the other fellow. One Friday he suggested that he and I might go to town on Saturday night for some fun. I jumped at the chance, of course, though I had no very clear idea of what fun he might be referring to. I warned him I didn't know how to dance; he said dancing was easy to learn. After dinner, must have been about seven-thirty, we headed out. Rufino had spruced himself up like a fellow on his way to a party, and he was sporting a knife with a silver handle; I left my little hatpin of a knife at home, for fear of being joshed some about it. It didn't take us long to come in sight of the first houses. Have any of you fellows ever been to Lobos? Just as well; there's not a town in the provinces that's not just like all the others—even to the point of thinking it's different. The same dirt streets with the same holes in them, the same squat houses—as though to make a man on horseback feel all the taller. We pulled up at this one corner in front of a house painted light blue or pink, with the name La Estrella painted on it. There were horses tied to the hitching post, with nice saddles, all of them. The front door was open a bit, and I could see a crack of light. Off the back of the vestibule there was a long room with plank benches all along the walls and between one bench and another all these dark doorways that led who knew where. An ugly little yellow dog scurried out yapping to make us feel welcome. There were quite a few people; half a dozen women wearing flowered housecoats were wandering around. A respectable-looking woman, dressed in black from head to toe, looked to me to be the owner of the house. Rufino walked up and said hello to her, then gestured toward me.

"I've brought you a new friend," he said, "but he's not much of a rider yet."

"He'll learn, don't worry your head about it," the lady replied. That abashed me, of course. To cover my embarrassment, or maybe to make them see I was just a boy, I sat down on the end of a bench and started playing with the dog. On the kitchen table they had lit some tallow candles stuck in bottles, and I also remember the little wood stove in one corner of the room, at the back. On the whitewashed wall in front of me was a figure of the Virgen de la Merced.

There was a good bit of joking, and somebody was strumming at a guitar—not that it did him much good. Out of sheer timidity, I didn't say no to the gin somebody offered me, which burned my mouth like red-hot coals. Among the women there was one that seemed different to me from the others. They called her the Captive. There was something kind of Indian-featured about her, but she was as pretty as a picture—that sad-eyed look, you know. Her hair was in a braid that reached all the way to her waist. Rufino saw that I was looking at her.

"Tell us that story about the Indian raid again, to freshen up our memories some," he said to her.

The way the girl talked, there mightn't have been another soul in the room, and somehow I got the feeling there was nothing else she could think about, that this was the only thing that had happened to her in her whole life. She told the story this way—

"When they brought me from Catamarca I was just a little girl. What could I know about Indian raids? On the ranch they were so afraid of them they wouldn't even mention them. Gradually I learned about the raids, almost like they were a secret that nobody was supposed to tell—how Indians might swarm down like a thundercloud and kill people and steal the animals. Women, they carried off to the interior, and did terrible things to them. I tried as hard as I could not to believe it. Lucas, my brother, who later got speared, swore it was all lies, but when something's true, you know it the first time you hear it. The government sends them things—tobacco, *mate*, liquor, *hierba*—to keep them quiet, but they have crafty leaders—spirit men—that warn them off it. If a chief of theirs orders it, they think nothing of storming down on a fort. The forts are scattered. . . . From thinking about it so much, I almost wished they'd come, and I would sit and look out in the direction where the sun goes down. I never learned about keeping track of time, but I do know there came frosts and summers and branding seasons and the death of the foreman's son, and then they did come. It was like the very wind off the pampas brought them. I saw a thistle flower in a ravine and I dreamed of the Indians. The next morning it happened. Like in an earthquake, the animals knew it before we did. The whole herd was skittish, and birds were flying through the air every which way. We ran to look out in the direction I always looked in . . ."

"Who brought you the warning?" somebody asked.

The girl still seemed far away. She just repeated her last words.

"We ran to look out in the direction I always looked in. It was like the whole desert had up and started moving. Through those thick rods of the wrought-iron fence we saw the dust clouds before we saw the Indians. They were on a raid. They were slapping their mouths with their hands and yelping. There were rifles in Santa Irene, but all they were good for was stunning them and making them all the madder."

The Captive's way of speaking was like a person saying a prayer, from memory; but out in the street I could hear the Indians coming across the plain, and their yelping. Then a door banged open, and they were in the room—you'd have thought they'd ridden their horses inside, into the rooms of a dream. It was a bunch of drunken brawlers from the docks. Now, in my memory's eye, they look very tall. The one in the lead gave Rufino, who was by the door, an elbow for his trouble. Rufino turned pale, said not a word, and stepped off to one side. The lady, who'd not moved from her place, stood up.

"It's Juan Moreira,*" she announced.

Here, tonight, after so many years, I'm not sure anymore whether I remember the man that was actually there that night or whether it's the man I was to see so many times afterward around

51

the slaughterhouses. I think about Podestá's long hair and black beard,* but there's also a blondish sort of face there somewhere, with smallpox scars. Anyway, that ugly dog skittered out yapping to greet the newcomers. With one crack of his bullwhip, Moreira laid it out dead on the floor. It fell over on its back and died waving its paws in the air. . . .

Now then, this is where the story really starts—

Without making a sound I crept over to one of the doors, which opened into a narrow hallway and a flight of stairs. Upstairs, I hid in a dark bedroom. Except for the bed, which was a low, squat affair, I couldn't say what sort of furniture there might have been. I was shaking all over. Downstairs there was yelling and shrieking, and then the sound of breaking glass. I heard a woman's footsteps coming up the stairs, and then I saw a slice of light. Then the voice of the Captive called me, almost in a whisper.

"I'm here to be of service, but only to peaceable folk. Come over here, I won't hurt you."

She had taken off her housecoat. I lay down beside her and took her face in my hands. I don't know how much time passed. There was not a word or a kiss between us. I undid her braid and played with her hair, which was long and straight, and then with her. We never saw each other again, and I never learned her name.

A gunshot stunned us.

"You can get out by the other staircase," the Captive told me.

Which is what I did, and I found myself out in the dirt street. There was a big moon that night. A police sergeant, carrying a rifle with fixed bayonet, was watching that side of the house. He laughed when he saw me.

"From all appearances," he said to me, "you like to get an early start in the morning."

I must have said something in return, but he paid me no further mind. A man was letting himself down the wall. In one movement, the sergeant ran him through with the bayonet. The man fell to the ground, where he lay on his back, whimpering and bleeding.

That dog came to my mind. The sergeant stabbed the man good with the bayonet again, to finish him off once and for all.

With a happy kind of grin he said to the man, "Moreira, this time you might as well have saved your powder."

The uniformed men who'd been surrounding the house appeared from everywhere, and then came the neighbors. Andrés Chirino had to wrestle the gun out of his hand. Everybody wanted to congratulate him.

Laughing, Rufino said, "I guess that'll be this hoodlum's last dance!"

I went from group to group, telling people what I had seen. Suddenly I was very tired; it may be I had a fever. I slipped away, found Rufino, and we started back home. From the horse we could see the white light of the dawn. More than tired, I felt dazed—as though I'd been caught up in a rapids.

"In the river of the events of that night," mused my father.

The other man nodded.

"That's it exactly. Within the space of a few hours I'd learned how to make love and I'd seen death at first hand. To all men all things are revealed—or at least all those things that a man's fated to know; but from sundown of one day to sunup of the next, those two central things were revealed to me. The years go by, and I've told the story so many times that I'm not sure anymore whether I actually remember it or whether I just remember the words I tell it with. Maybe that's how it was with the Captive, with her Indian raid. At this point what difference does it make whether it was me or some other man that saw Moreira killed?"

The Mirror and the Mask

When the armies clashed at the Battle of Clontarf, in which the Norwegian was brought low, the king spoke to his poet and said:

"The brightest deeds lose their luster if they are not minted in words. I desire you to sing my victory and my praises. I shall be Æneas; you shall be my Virgil. Do you believe you have the gifts worthy of this task I ask of you, which shall make us both immortal?"

"Yes, great king, I do," answered the poet. "I am Olan. For twelve winters I have honed my skills at meter. I know by heart the three hundred sixty fables which are the foundation of all true poetry. The Ulster cycle and the Munster cycle lie within my harp strings. I am licensed by law to employ the most archaic words of the language, and its most complex metaphors. I have mastered the secret script which guards our art from the prying eyes of the common folk. I can sing of love, of cattle theft, of sailing ships, of war. I know the mythological lineage of all the royal houses of Ireland. I possess the secret knowledge of herbs, astrology, mathematics, and canon law. I have defeated my rivals in public contest. I have trained myself in satire, which causes diseases of the skin, including leprosy. And I also wield the sword, as I have proven in your battle. There is but one thing that I do not know: how to express my thanks for this gift you make me."

The high king, who was easily wearied by other men's long speeches, said to the poet with relief:

"All these things I know full well. I have just been told that the nightingale has now sung in England. When the rains and snow have passed, when the nightingale has returned from its journey to the lands of the south, you shall recite your verses before the court and the Guild of Poets assembled. I give you one full year. Every letter and every word, you shall burnish to a fine gleam. The recompense, as you know, shall not be unworthy of my royal wont, nor of the hours you spend in sleepless inspiration."

"My lord, my greatest recompense is the sight of your face," said the poet, who was something of a courtier as well.

He bowed and retired, a verse or two already beginning to creep into his head.

When the allotted period had passed, a time filled with plague and rebellion, the panegyric was sung. The poet declaimed his verses with slow assurance, and without a glance at his manuscript. In the course of it, the king often nodded approvingly. Everyone imitated his gesture, even those who, crowding in at the doors, could not make out a word of it.

At last the king spoke.

"I accept this labor. It is another victory. You have given to each word its true meaning, to each noun the epithet bestowed upon it by the first poets. In all the work there is not an image which the classics did not employ. War is 'the fair cloth wov'n of men' and blood is 'sword-drink.' The sea has its god and the clouds foretell the future. You have marshaled rhyme, alliteration, assonance, scansion, the artifices of erudite rhetoric, the wise alternation of meters, and all with greatest skillfulness. If the whole of the literature of Ireland should—*omen absit*—be lost, well might it all be reconstructed, without loss, from your classic ode. Thirty scribes shall transcribe it, twelve times each."

There was a silence. Then the king went on:

"All that is well, and yet nothing has happened. In our veins the blood has beat no faster. Our hands have not gone for our bows. No one's cheeks have paled. No one has bellowed out a battle cry, no one has stood to meet the Viking attack. In one year, poet, we shall gather to applaud another poem. As a sign of our thanks, take this mirror, which is of silver."

"I thank you," said the poet, "and I understand and obey."

The stars of the sky once more journeyed their bright course. Once more sang the nightingale in the Saxon forests, and the poet returned with his scroll—shorter this time than before. He did not recite it from memory; he read it, visibly unsure, omitting certain passages, as though he himself did not entirely understand them, or did not wish to profane them. The verses were strange. They were not a description of the battle, they were the battle. In the warlike chaos of the lines there stirred the God Who Is Three Yet One, the pagan noumena of Ireland, and those who would war, centuries after, at the beginning of the Elder Edda. The poem's form was no less strange. A singular noun might govern a plural verb. The prepositions were foreign to common usage. Harshness vied with sweetness. The metaphors were arbitrary, or so they seemed.

The king exchanged a few words with the men of letters assembled about him, and he spoke in this way:

"Of your first hymn I was able to say that it was a happy summation of all that has been written in Ireland. *This* poem surpasses all that has gone before, and obliterates it. It holds one in thrall, it thrills, it dazzles. It will pass over the heads of the ignorant, and their praises will not be yours, but the praises of the few, the learned—ah! An ivory chest shall hold the only copy. From the pen that has penned such a lofty work, we may expect one that is more elevated yet. . . ."

Then he added, smiling:

"We are figures in a fable, and it is only right that we recall that in fables, the number three is first above all others."

"The three gifts of the wizard, the triads, and the indubitable Trinity," was all that the poet dared allow himself to murmur.

The king went on:

"As a token of our thanks, take this mask. It is of gold."

"I thank you, and I understand and obey," the poet said.

The anniversary returned. The palace sentinels noticed that this time the poet did not bring a manuscript. Not without dismay did the king look upon the poet: he was greatly changed. Something, which was not simply time, had furrowed and transformed his features. His eyes seemed to stare far into the distance, or to have been rendered blind. The poet begged to be allowed to speak to the king. The slaves cleared the hall.

"Have you not composed the ode?" asked the king.

"I have," said the poet sadly. "Would that Christ our Lord had forbade it."

"Can you recite it?"

"I dare not."

"I charge you with the courage that you need," the king declared.

The poet spoke the poem. It was a single line.

Unable to summon the courage to speak it again aloud, the poet and his king mouthed the poem, as though it were a secret supplication, or a blasphemy. The king was no less astounded and cowed than the poet. The two men, very pale, looked at each other.

"In the years of my youth," said the king, "I sailed toward the setting sun. On an island there, I saw silver greyhounds that hunted golden boars to their death. On another we were feted with the fragrance of magic apples. On yet another I saw walls of fire. On the most remote of all, there was a vaulted river that hung from the sky, and in its waters swam fish and sailing ships. Those were marvels, but they do not compare with your poem, which somehow contains them all. What sorcery has given you this?"

"At dawn," said this poet, "I awoke speaking words that at first I did not understand. Those words are the poem. I felt I had committed some sin, perhaps that sin which the Holy Spirit cannot pardon."

"The sin the two of us now share," mused the king. "The sin

of having known Beauty, which is a gift forbidden mankind. Now we must atone for it. I gave you a mirror and a golden mask; here is the third gift, which shall be the last."

He laid in the poet's right hand a dagger.

Of the poet, we know that he killed himself when he left the palace; of the king, that he is a beggar who wanders the roads of Ireland, which once was his kingdom, and that he has never spoken the poem again.

"Undr"

I must inform the reader that the pages I translate and publish here will be sought in vain in the *Libellus* (1615) of Adam of Bremen, who, as we all know, was born and died in the eleventh century. Lappenberg found the text within a manuscript in the Bodleian, at Oxford; given its wealth of circumstantial detail, he judged it to be a late interpolation, but he did publish it as a curiosity in his *Analecta Germanica* (Leipzig, 1894). The opinion of a mere Argentine *amateur* is worth very little; readers may judge these pages as they will. My translation is not literal, but it is faithful.

Thus writes Adam of Bremen:

. . . Of the several nations that border the wide desert which lies on the far shore of the Gulf, beyond the lands where the wild horse mates, that one most worthy of mention is the nation of the Urns. The imprecise or fabulous reports of merchants, the difficulty of the road, and the depredations of nomads prevented me from ever reaching its borders. I know, however, that its precarious and remote villages lie within the lowlands of the Wisla River. Unlike the Swedes, the Urns profess the true faith in Christ, unsullied by the Arianism and bloody worship of devils from which the royal houses of England and the other nations of the North draw their lineage. They are shepherds, ferrymen, sorcerers, swordsmiths, and ropemakers. The severity of their wars almost entirely prevents them from tilling their lands. The plains and the tribes that roam them have made the Urns skillful with horse and bow. In time, one inevitably comes to resemble one's enemies. Their lances are longer than ours, for theirs are made for horsemen, not for infantry.

As one might imagine, the use of pen, inkhorn, and parchment is unknown to them. They carve their characters in stone, as our forebears carved the runes revealed to them by Odin, after having hung from the ash tree—Odin sacrificed to Odin—for nine long nights.

To these general bits of knowledge I will add the story of my conversation with the Icelander Ulf Sigurdarson, a man of grave and measured speech. We had met in Uppsala, near the temple. The wood fire had died; the cold and the dawn light were seeping in through the uneven chinks in the walls. Outside, the gray wolves that devour the flesh of pagans sacrificed to the three gods were leaving their cautious spoor upon the snow. Our talk had begun in Latin, as is the habit between members of the clergy, but soon we had passed into the language of the North, known from Ultima Thule to the markets of Asia. This is what the man told me:

"I am of the line of *skalds*; the moment I learned that the poetry of the Urns is a poetry of a single word, I went in quest of them, in quest of the route that would lead me to their land. Not without weariness and labor did I reach it, one year later. It was night; I noticed that the men I met along my way regarded me curiously, and I could not fail to note that I was struck by an occasional stone. I saw the glow of a smith's forge, and I entered.

"The smith offered me shelter for the night. His name, he said, was Orm, and his language was more or less our own. We exchanged a few words. It was from his lips that I first heard the name of the king who then ruled over them—Gunnlaug. I learned that he had fought in their last war, that he looked with suspicion upon foreigners, and that it was his custom to crucify them. In order to avoid that fate, which was more fitting for a God than

for a man, I undertook to write a *drápa*, a laudatory composition—
a sort of eulogy praising the king's victories, his fame, and his
mercy. No sooner had I committed the poem to memory than
two men came for me. I refused to relinquish my sword, but I
allowed myself to be led away.

"The stars were still in the sky. We traveled through a stretch
of land with huts scattered here and there along the way. I had
heard tales of pyramids; what I saw in the first square we came to
was a stake of yellow wood. On its sharp point I could make out
the black figure of a fish. Orm, who had accompanied us, told me
that the fish was the Word. In the next square I saw a red stake,
with a disk. Orm said once more that this was the Word. I asked
him to tell me what word it was; he replied that he was but a
simple artisan, and did not know.

"In the third square, which was the last, I saw a stake painted
black, bearing a design I no longer remember. On the far side of
the square there was a long straight wall, whose ends I could not
see. I later found that it was circular, roofed with clay, without
interior doors, and that it girded the entire city. The horses tied
to a wooden post were compact and thick-maned.

"The smith was not allowed to enter. There were armed men
inside, all standing. Gunnlaug, the king, who was suffering under
some great affliction, was lying with half-closed eyes upon a kind
of dais; his pallet was of camel skins. He was a worn, yellow man,
a sacred and almost forgotten object; long, time-blurred scars
made a tracery across his chest. One of the soldiers made way for
me. Someone had brought a harp. I knelt and softly intoned the
drápa. It was adorned with the tropes, alliterations, and accents
required by the genre. I am not certain that the king understood
it, but he gave me a silver ring, which I still possess. Under his
pillow I glimpsed the blade of a dagger. To his right there was a
chessboard of a hundred or more squares and several scattered
pieces.

"The king's guards pushed me back. A man took my place, but

he stood as he offered his own poem. He plucked at the harp's strings as though tuning them, and then very softly repeated the word that I wish I might have caught, but did not. Someone reverently said *Now, meaningless.*

"I saw tears here and there. The man would raise his voice or it would grow distant; the nearly identical chords were monotonous, or, more precisely, infinite. I wished the chant could go on forever, I wished it were my life. Suddenly, it ended. I heard the sound of the harp when the singer, no doubt exhausted, cast it to the floor. We made our way in disorder from the room. I was one of the last. I saw with astonishment that the light was fading.

"I walked a few steps. A hand upon my shoulder detained me. A voice said to me:

"'The king's ring was a talisman bestowed upon you, yet soon your death shall come, for you have heard the Word. I, Bjarni Thorkelsson, will save you. I am of the lineage of the *skalds*. In your dithyramb you called blood "sword-drink" and battle "man-battle." I remember hearing those tropes from my father's father. You and I are poets; I shall save you. Now we do not name every thing or event that fires our song; we encode it in a single word, which is the Word.'

"'I could not hear it,' I replied to him. 'I beg you to tell me what word it is.'

"He hesitated for a moment, and then said:

"'I am sworn not to reveal it. And besides, no one can teach another anything. You must seek it on your own. We must hurry, for your life is in danger. I will hide you in my house, where they will not dare come to look for you. If the wind is with you, you shall sail tomorrow to the South.'

"Thus began the adventure that was to last for so many winters. I shall not tell its hazards, nor shall I attempt to recall the true order of its vicissitudes. I was oarsman, slave merchant, slave, woodcutter, robber of caravans, cantor, assayer of deep water and of metals. I suffered a year's captivity in the mercury mines, which loosens the teeth. I fought with men from Sweden in the militia of Mikligarthr—Constantinople. On the banks of the Azov I was loved by a woman I shall never forget; I left her, or she left me, which is the same. I betrayed and was betrayed. More than once fate made me kill. A Greek soldier challenged me to fight him, and offered me the choice of two swords. One was a handspan longer than the other. I realized that he was trying to intimidate me, so I chose the shorter. He asked me why. I told him that the distance from my hand to his heart did not vary. On the shore of the Black Sea sits the runic epitaph I carved for my comrade Leif Arnarson. I have fought with the Blue Men of Serkland, the Saracens. In the course of time I have been many men, but that whirlwind of events was one long dream. The essential thing always was the Word. There were times when I did not believe in it. I would tell myself that renouncing the lovely game of combining lovely words was foolish, that there was no reason to seek the single, perhaps illusory, One. That argument failed. A missionary suggested the word *God*, which I rejected. One sunrise, on the banks of a river that widened into the sea, I believed that the revelation had been vouchsafed me.

"I returned to the land of the Urns, and with difficulty found the poet's house.

"I entered and said my name. Night had fallen. Thorkelsson, from his place upon the ground, told me to light the candle in the bronze candelabrum. His face had aged so greatly that I could not help thinking that I myself was now old. As was the custom, I asked after the health of the king.

"'His name is no longer Gunnlaug,' he replied. 'Now his name is other. Tell me of your travels.'

"I did so in the best order I could, and in verbose detail, which I shall here omit. Before I came to the end, the poet interrupted me.

"'Did you often sing in those lands?' he asked.

"The question took me by surprise.

"'At first,' I said, 'I sang to earn my bread. Then, from a fear that I do not understand, I grew distant from the singing and the harp.'

"'Hmm.' He nodded. 'Now, go on with your story.'

"I complied. Then there fell a long silence.

"'What were you given by the first woman you slept with?' he asked.

"'Everything,' I answered.

"'I, too, have been given everything, by life. Life gives all men everything, but most men do not know this. My voice is tired and my fingers weak, but listen to me. . . .'

"He spoke the word *Undr*, which means *wonder*.

"I was overwhelmed by the song of the man who lay dying, but in his song, and in his chord, I saw my own labors, the slave girl who had given me her first love, the men I had killed, the cold dawns, the northern lights over the water, the oars. I took up the harp and sang—a different word.

"'Hmm,' said the poet, and I had to draw close to hear him. 'You have understood me.'"

A Weary Man's Utopia

He called it "Utopia," a Greek word which means "there is no such place."   Quevedo

No two mountain peaks are alike, but anywhere on earth the plains are one and the same. I was riding down a road across the plains. I asked myself without much curiosity whether I was in Oklahoma or Texas or the region that literary men call "the pampas." There was not a fence to left or right. As on other occasions, I slowly murmured these lines, more or less from Emilio Oribe:

> *Riding through the ongoing, ongoing and interminable*
> *Terrifying plains, near the frontier of Brazil . . .*

The road was rutted and uneven. Rain began to fall. Some two or three hundred yards down the road, I saw the light of a house. It was squat and rectangular and surrounded by trees. The door was opened by a man so tall it almost frightened me. He was dressed in gray. I sensed that he was waiting for someone. There was no latch or lock on the door.

We went inside, into a long room with walls of exposed wood. From the ceiling hung a lamp that gave a yellowish light. The table seemed odd, somehow. There was a water clock on the table, the first I'd ever seen, save for the occasional steel engraving in dictionaries and encyclopedias. The man motioned me to one of the chairs.

I tried several languages, but we couldn't make ourselves understood to each other. When he spoke, it was in Latin. I gathered my recollections of my distant student days and girded myself for conversation.

"By your clothing," he said, "I can see that you have come from another time. The diversity of languages encouraged the diversity of nations, and even encouraged war; the earth has returned to Latin. There are those who fear that it will degenerate into French, Limousine, or Papiamento, but the danger is not imminent. And in any case, neither that which has been nor that which is to be holds any interest for me."

I said nothing; the man went on.

"If it does not repulse you to see another person eat, would you like to join me?"

I realized that he had seen that I was at an utter loss, so I said I would.

We went down a corridor with several doors leading off it and came into a small kitchen in which everything was made of metal. We returned to the first room with our dinner on a tray: bowls of cornflakes, a bunch of grapes, a fruit that was unknown to me but whose taste was something like a fig, and a large pitcher of water. I don't believe there was any bread. My host's features were sharp, and there was something peculiar about his eyes. I shall never forget that stern, pale face that I shall never see again. He did not gesture with his hands when he talked.

I was a bit tongue-tied by having to speak Latin, but at last I said:

"You are not astounded by my sudden appearance here?"

"No," he replied, "every century or so we receive these visits. They do not last long; you will be back home by tomorrow, at the latest."

The certainty in his voice relieved me. I thought it proper to introduce myself:

"I am Eudoro Acevedo. I was born in 1897 in the city of Buenos

Aires. I am now seventy years old, a professor of English and American literature and a writer of tales of fantasy."

"I remember having read without displeasure," he said, "two tales of fantasy—the Travels of Captain Lemuel Gulliver, which many people believe to have really taken place, and the *Summa Theologica*. But let us not talk of facts. No one cares about facts anymore. They are mere points of departure for speculation and exercises in creativity. In school we are taught Doubt, and the Art of Forgetting—especially forgetting all that is personal and local. We live in time, which is successive, but we try to live *sub specie æternitatis*. There are a few names from the past that are still with us, though the language tends to forget them. We avoid pointless precision. There is no chronology or history; no statistics, either. You told me your name is Eudoro; I cannot tell you mine, because everyone calls me 'somebody' or 'you.'"

"But what was your father's name?"

"He had none."

On one of the walls I noticed a bookshelf. I opened a volume at random; the letters were clear and indecipherable and written by hand. Their angular lines reminded me of the runic alphabet, though it had been used only for inscriptions. It occurred to me that the people of the future were not only taller, they were more skilled as well. I instinctively looked at the man's long elegant fingers.

"Now," he said to me, "you are going to see something you have never seen before."

He carefully handed me a copy of More's *Utopia*, the volume printed in Basel in 1518; some pages and illustrations were missing.

It was not without some smugness that I replied:

"It is a printed book. I have more than two thousand at home, though they are not as old or as valuable."

I read the title aloud.

The man laughed.

"No one can read two thousand books. In the four hundred

years I have lived, I've not read more than half a dozen. And in any case, it is not the reading that matters, but the rereading. Printing, which is now forbidden, was one of the worst evils of mankind, for it tended to multiply unnecessary texts to a dizzying degree."

"In that strange yesterday from which I have come," I replied, "there prevailed the superstition that between one evening and the next morning, events occur that it would be shameful to have no knowledge of. The planet was peopled by spectral collectives—Canada, Brazil, the Swiss Congo, the Common Market. Almost no one knew the prior history of those Platonic entities, yet everyone was informed of the most trivial details of the latest conference of pedagogues or the imminent breaking off of relations between one of these entities and another and the messages that their presidents sent back and forth—composed by a secretary to the secretary, and in the prudent vagueness that the form requires.

"All this was no sooner read than forgotten, for within a few hours it would be blotted out by new trivialities. Of all functions, that of the politician was without doubt the most public. An ambassador or a minister was a sort of cripple who had to be transported in long, noisy vehicles surrounded by motorcyclists and grenadiers and stalked by eager photographers. One would have thought their feet had been cut off, my mother used to say. Images and the printed word were more real than things. People believed only what they could read on the printed page. The principle, means, and end of our singular conception of the world was *esse est percipi*—'to be is to be portrayed.' In the past I lived in, people were credulous; they believed that a piece of merchandise was good because the manufacturer of that piece of merchandise said it was. Robbery was also a frequent occurrence, though everyone knew that the possession of money brings with it neither greater happiness nor greater peace of mind."

"Money?" my host repeated. "No one any longer suffers poverty, which must have been unbearable—nor suffers wealth, for that matter, which must have been the most uncomfortable form of vulgarity. Every person now has a job to perform."

"Like rabbis," I said.

He seemed not to understand; he continued on.

"There are no cities, either. To judge by the ruins of Bahía Blanca,* which curiosity once led me to explore, it's no great loss. Since there are no possessions, there is no inheritance. When a man reaches a hundred years of age, he is ready to confront himself and his solitude. He will have engendered one child."

"One child?" I asked.

"Yes. One. It is not advisable that the human race be too much encouraged. There are those who think that awareness of the universe is a faculty that comes from the deity, yet no one knows for a certainty whether this deity exists. I believe that what is being discussed now is the advantages and disadvantages of the gradual or simultaneous suicide of every person on earth. But let us return to the matter at hand."

I nodded.

"When the individual has reached a hundred years of age, he is able to do without love and friendship. Illness and inadvertent death are not things to be feared. He practices one of the arts, or philosophy or mathematics, or plays a game of one-handed chess. When he wishes, he kills himself. When a man is the master of his own life, he is also the master of his death."

"Is that a quotation?" I asked.

"Of course. There is nothing but quotations left for us. Our language is a system of quotations."

"What about the great adventure of my times—space travel?" I asked.

"It's been hundreds of years since we have done any of that traveling about—though it was undoubtedly admirable. We found we could never escape the here and now."

Then, with a smile he added:

"And besides, every journey is a journey through space. Going from one planet to another is much like going to the farm across the way. When you stepped into this room, you were engaging in space travel."

"That's true," I replied. "There was also much talk of 'chemical substances' and 'zoological animals.'"

The man now turned his back to me and looked out the windows. Outside, the plains were white with silent snow and moonlight.

I emboldened myself to ask:

"Are there still museums and libraries?"

"No. We want to forget the past, save for the composition of elegies. There are no commemorations or anniversaries or portraits of dead men. Each person must produce on his own the arts and sciences that he has need for."

"In that case, every man must be his own Bernard Shaw, his own Jesus Christ, and his own Archimedes."

He nodded wordlessly.

"What happened to the governments?" I inquired.

"It is said that they gradually fell into disuse. Elections were called, wars were declared, taxes were levied, fortunes were confiscated, arrests were ordered, and attempts were made at imposing censorship—but no one on the planet paid any attention. The press stopped publishing pieces by those it called its 'contributors,' and also publishing their obituaries. Politicians had to find honest work; some became comedians, some witch doctors—some excelled at those occupations. The reality was no doubt more complex than this summary."

Then his tone changed, and he said:

"I have built this house, which is like all other houses. I have built these furnishings and made these household goods. I have worked in the fields, though other men, whose faces I have not seen, may well have worked them better. I can show you some things."

I followed him into an adjoining room. He lighted a lamp, which also hung from the ceiling. In one corner I saw a harp; it had very few strings. On the walls hung rectangular paintings in which the color yellow predominated. They did not look as if the same hand had painted them all.

"This is my work," he said.

I examined the paintings, and I stopped before the smallest of them, which portrayed, or suggested, a sunset, though there was something of the infinite about it.

"If you like it, you may take it back with you, as a souvenir of a future friend," he said serenely.

I thanked him, but the other canvases disturbed me. I will not say that they were blank, but they were almost blank.

"They are painted with colors that your ancient eyes cannot see."

His delicate hands plucked the strings of the harp and I could hear faint occasional notes.

It was then that the banging began.

A tall woman and three or four men came into the house. One would have said they were brothers and sister, or that time had made them resemble one another. My host spoke first to the woman:

"I knew you would not fail to come tonight. Have you seen Nils?"

"Every few evenings. He is still mad about painting."

"Let us hope he has better luck at it than his father had."

Manuscripts, paintings, furniture, household goods—we left nothing in the house.

The woman worked as hard as the men. I felt embarrassed at my own weakness, which kept me from being much help to them. No one closed the door as, loaded down with our burden, we left. I noticed that the house had a peaked roof.

After about fifteen minutes of walking, we turned toward the left. In the distance I saw a kind of tower, crowned with a dome.

"It is the crematory," someone said. "The death chamber is inside. They say it was invented by a philanthropist whose name, I believe, was Adolf Hitler."

The caretaker, whose height did not take me aback, opened the gate to us.

My host whispered a few words. Before going in, he waved good-bye.

"There'll be more snow," the woman announced.

In my study on Calle México still hangs the canvas that someone will paint, thousands of years from now, with substances that are now scattered across the planet.

The Bribe

The story I shall tell is about two men, or rather about an incident in which two men played a part. The event, which is not at all singular or fantastic, is less important than the character of the two men involved. Both were vain, though in very different ways and with very different results. The anecdote (for it's really very little more than that) took place a short time ago in one of the states of the United States. In my opinion, it couldn't have happened anywhere else.

In late 1961, at the University of Texas in Austin, I was fortunate enough to have a long conversation with one of the two men, Dr. Ezra Winthrop. Dr. Winthrop was a professor of Old English (he did not approve of calling it Anglo-Saxon, which suggests an artifact cobbled together out of two separate pieces). I recall that without ever actually contradicting me he corrected my many errors and presumptuous temerities. I was told that on oral examinations he never put questions to the candidate—instead he invited the candidate to chat about this or that subject, leaving to the person being examined the choice of the topic to be discussed. Of old Puritan stock, a native of Boston, he'd found it hard to adapt to the customs and prejudices of the south. He missed the snow, but I've noticed that northerners are taught to take measures against the cold the way we are against the heat. The hazy image that remains to me is that of a man on the tall side, with gray hair, less spry than strong. My recollection of his colleague Herbert Locke is clearer; Locke gave me a copy of his book *Toward a*

History of the Kenning, which declares that the Saxons soon put
aside those somewhat mechanical metaphors they used (the sea
as "whale-road," the eagle as "battle-falcon"), while the Scandinavian poets were combining and intermingling them almost to
the point of inextricability. I mention Herbert Locke because he
is an integral part of my story.

I come now to the Icelander Eric Einarsson, perhaps the true
protagonist. I never saw him. He had come to Texas in 1969,
when I was in Cambridge, but letters from a mutual friend, Ramón
Martínez López, have left me with the conviction that I knew
him intimately. I know that he is impetuous, energetic, and cold;
in a land of tall men he is tall. Given his red hair, it was inevitable
that students should start calling him Eric the Red. It was his view
that the use of an inevitably error-ridden slang makes the foreigner
an interloper, and so he never condescended to use the ubiquitous
"O.K." A fine scholar of English, Latin, the Scandinavian languages, and (though he wouldn't admit it) German, he easily
made a way for himself in American universities. His first article
was a monograph on the four articles de Quincey had written on
the influence of the Danes on the lake region of Westmoreland.
This was followed by a second, on the dialect of the Yorkshire
peasant. Both studies were well received, but Einarsson thought
his career needed something a bit more "astonishing." In 1970,
Yale published his copiously annotated critical edition of the
ballad of the Battle of Maldon. The scholarship of the notes was
undeniable, but certain hypotheses in the introduction aroused
some controversy in the virtually hermetic spheres of academe.
Einarsson claimed, for example, that the style of the ballad is
similar, though admittedly in a distant sort of way, to the epic
fragment *Finnsburh,* rather than to the measured rhetoric of *Beowulf,* and that the poem's employment of moving circumstantial
details oddly prefigures the methods that we admire, not without
good reason, in the Icelandic sagas. He also proposed emendations
for several readings in Elphinston's edition. In 1969 he had been

given an appointment at the University of Texas. As we all know, American universities are forever sponsoring conferences of Germanists. Dr. Winthrop had chaired the previous conference, in East Lansing. The head of his department, who was preparing to go abroad on his sabbatical, asked Winthrop to suggest a person to chair the next one, in Wisconsin. There were really only two candidates to choose between—Herbert Locke and Eric Einarsson.

Winthrop, like Carlyle, had renounced the Puritan faith of his forebears, but not their sense of right and wrong. He did not decline to offer his opinion; his duty was clear. Since 1954 Herbert Locke had been of inestimable help in the preparation of a certain annotated edition of *Beowulf* which, at certain institutions of higher learning, had replaced that of Klaeber; he was now compiling a work that would be of great usefulness to Germanists: an English/Anglo-Saxon dictionary that was certain to save readers hours of often fruitless searching through etymological dictionaries. Einarsson was much the younger. His sharpness and impertinence had won him general dislike, including Winthrop's, but his critical edition of *Finnsburh* had contributed not a little to building a reputation. And he was disputatious; at the conference he would be a better moderator than the shy and taciturn Locke. That was the state of Winthrop's deliberations when the incident occurred.

From the Yale press there appeared a long article on the teaching of Anglo-Saxon language and literature in universities. At the end of the last page appeared the transparent initials *E.E.* and, to dispel any doubt as to the authorship, the words "*University of Texas.*" The article, written in the correct English of a nonnative speaker, never stooped to incivility, yet it did have a certain belligerence about it. It argued that beginning the study of Anglo-Saxon with *Beowulf*, a work of ancient date but a rhetorical, pseudo-Virgilian style, was no less arbitrary than beginning the study of English with the intricate verses of Milton. It advised that chronological order be inverted: begin with the eleventh-century poem "The Grave," through which something of the modern-day language might be glimpsed, and then work backward to the beginnings. As for *Beowulf*, some fragment excerpted from the tedious 3000-line amalgam would suffice—the funerary rites of the Scyld, for example, who returned to the sea as they had come from the sea. Not once was Winthrop's name mentioned, but Winthrop felt persistently attacked. The attack, if there was one, mattered less to him than the fact that his pedagogical methods were being impugned.

There were but a few days left. Winthrop wanted to be fair, and he could not allow Einarsson's article (already being reread and talked about by many people) to influence his decision. But the decision was not easy. One morning Winthrop spoke with his director; that same afternoon, Einarsson received official word that he would be going to Wisconsin to chair the conference.

On the day before the nineteenth of March, the day of his departure, Einarsson appeared in Ezra Winthrop's office. He had come to say good-bye and to thank him. One of the windows overlooked a diagonal, tree-lined walk, and the office was lined with books. Einarsson immediately recognized the parchment-bound first edition of the *Edda Islandorum*. Winthrop replied that he knew Einarsson would carry out his mission well, and that he had nothing to thank him for. The conversation was, unless I am mistaken, a long one.

"Let's speak frankly," Einarsson said. "There's not a soul in this university that doesn't know that it is on your recommendation that Dr. Lee Rosenthal, our director, has honored me with the mission of representing our university. I will try not to disappoint him. I am a good Germanist; the language of the sagas is the language of my childhood, and I speak Anglo-Saxon better than my British colleagues. My students say *cyning*, not *cunning*. They also know that they are absolutely forbidden to smoke in class and that they cannot come in dressed like hippies. As for my frustrated rival, it would be the worst of bad taste for me to criticize him;

the *Kenning* book clearly shows that he has looked into not only the primary sources but the pertinent articles by Meissner and Marquardt as well. But let us not pursue those trivialities.

"I owe you an explanation, Dr. Winthrop. I left my homeland in late 1967. When a man decides to leave his country and go to a distant land, he inevitably assumes the burden of 'getting ahead' in that new place. My first two little articles, which were strictly philological, were written for reasons other than to prove my ability. That, clearly, would not be enough. I had always been interested in 'Maldon,' which except for an occasional stumble I can recite from memory. I managed to persuade Yale to publish my critical edition. The ballad, as you know, records a Scandinavian victory, but as to my claim that it influenced the later Icelandic sagas, I believe that to be an absurd and even unthinkable idea. I included it in order to flatter English readers.

"I come now to the essential point—my controversial note in the *Yale Monthly*. As you must surely be aware, it presents, or attempts to present, the case for my approach to the subject, but it deliberately exaggerates the shortcomings in yours, which, in exchange for subjecting students to the tedium of three thousand consecutive complex verses that narrate a confused story, provides them with a large vocabulary that will allow them to enjoy— if by then they have not abandoned it—the entire corpus of Anglo-Saxon literature. Going to Wisconsin was my real goal. You and I, my dear friend, know that conferences are silly, that they require pointless expenditures, but that they are invaluable to one's *curriculum vitæ*."

Winthrop looked at him quizzically. He was intelligent, but he tended to take things seriously, including conferences and the universe, which could well be a cosmic joke.

"Perhaps you recall our first conversation," Einarsson went on. "I had just arrived from New York. It was a Sunday; the university dining hall was closed so we went over to the Nighthawk to have lunch. I learned many things that day. Like all good Europeans, I had always assumed that the Civil War was a crusade against slavery; you argued that the South had had a right to secede from the Union and maintain its own institutions. To make your arguments all the more forceful, you told me that you yourself were from the North and that one of your forebears had fought in the ranks with Henry Halleck. But you also praised the bravery of the Confederate troops. Unlike most men, I can grasp almost immediately what sort of person the other person is. That lunch was all I needed. I realized, my dear Winthrop, that you are ruled by that curious American passion for impartiality. You wish above all else to be 'fair-minded.' Precisely because you are from the North, you tried to understand and defend the South's cause. The moment I discovered that my trip to Wisconsin depended upon your recommendation to Rosenthal, I decided to take advantage of my little discovery. I realized that calling into question the methodology that you always use in your classes was the most effective way of winning your support. I wrote my article that very day. The submissions criteria for the journal specify that articles may be signed only with initials, but I did everything within my power to remove any doubt as to the author's identity. I even told many colleagues that I had written it."

There was a long silence. Winthrop was the first to break it.

"Now I see," he said. "I'm an old friend of Herbert's, whose work I admire; you attacked me, directly or indirectly. Refusing to recommend you would have been a kind of reprisal. I compared the merits of the two of you and the result was . . . well, we both know what the result was, don't we?"

He then added, as though thinking out loud:

"I may have given in to the vanity of not being vengeful. As you see, your stratagem worked."

"'Stratagem' is the proper word for it," replied Einarsson, "but I do not apologize for what I did. I acted in the best interests of our institution. I had decided to go to Wisconsin come what might."

"My first Viking," said Winthrop, looking him in the eye.

"Another romantic superstition. It isn't Scandinavian blood that makes a man a Viking. My forebears were good ministers of the evangelical church; at the beginning of the tenth century, my ancestors were perhaps good solid priests of Thor. In my family, so far as I know, there has never been a man of the sea."

"In mine there have been many," Winthrop replied. "Yet perhaps we aren't so different, you and I. We share one sin, at least—vanity. You've come to my office to throw in my face your ingenious stratagem; I gave you my support so I could boast of my integrity."

"But there is something else," Einarsson responded. "Our nationality. I am an American citizen. My destiny lies here, not in Ultima Thule. You will no doubt contend that a passport does not change a man's nature."

They shook hands and said good-bye.

Avelino Arredondo

The incident occurred in Montevideo in 1897.

Every Saturday the friends took the same table, off to one side, in the Café del Globo, like the poor honest men they were, knowing they cannot invite their friends home, or perhaps escaping it. They were all from Montevideo; at first it had been hard to make friends with Arredondo, a man from the interior who didn't allow confidences or ask questions. He was hardly more than twenty, a lean, dark-skinned young man, a bit on the short side, and perhaps a little clumsy. His face would have been anonymous had it not been rescued by his eyes, which were both sleepy and full of energy. He was a clerk in a dry goods store on Calle Buenos Aires, and he studied law in his spare time. When the others condemned the war that was ravaging the country* and that the president (so general opinion believed) was waging for reprehensible reasons, Arredondo remained silent. He also remained silent when the others laughed at him and called him a tightwad.

A short time after the Battle of Cerros Blancos,* Arredondo told his friends that they wouldn't be seeing him for a while; he had to go to Mercedes. The news disturbed no one. Someone told him to watch out for Aparicio Saravia's gang of gauchos*; Arredondo smiled and said he wasn't afraid of the Whites. His interlocutor, who had joined the party, said nothing.

It was harder to say good-bye to Clara, his sweetheart. He did it with almost the same words. He told her not to expect a letter, since he was going to be very, very busy. Clara, who was not in the habit of writing, accepted the condition without protest. The two young people loved each other very much.

Arredondo lived on the outskirts. He had a black servant woman with the same last name as his; her forebears had been slaves of the family back in the time of the Great War. She was a woman of absolute trustworthiness; Arredondo instructed her to tell anyone asking for him that he was away in the country. He had picked up his last wages at the dry goods store.

He moved into a room at the back of the house, the room that opened onto the patio of packed earth. The step was pointless, but it helped him begin that reclusion that his will imposed on him.

From the narrow iron bed in which he gradually recovered his habit of taking an afternoon siesta, he looked with some sadness upon an empty bookcase. He had sold all his books, even the volumes of the Introduction to Law. All he had kept was a Bible, which he had never read and never managed to finish.

He went through it page by page, sometimes with interest and sometimes with boredom, and he set himself the task of memorizing an occasional chapter of Exodus and the last of Ecclesiastes. He did not try to understand what he was reading. He was a freethinker, but he let not a night go by without repeating the Lord's Prayer, as he'd promised his mother when he came to Montevideo—breaking that filial promise might bring bad luck.

He knew that his goal was the morning of August 25. He knew exactly how many days he had to get through. Once he'd reached his goal, time would cease, or rather nothing that happened afterward would matter. He awaited the day like a man waiting for his joy and his liberation. He had stopped his watch so he wouldn't always be looking at it, but every night, when he heard the dark, far-off sound of the twelve chimes, he would pull a page off the calendar and think *One day less.*

At first he tried to construct a routine. Drink some *mate*, smoke the black cigarettes he rolled, read and review a certain number of pages, try to chat a bit with Clementina when she brought his dinner on a tray, repeat and embellish a certain speech before he blew out the lamp. Talking with Clementina, a woman along in years, was not easy, because her memory had halted far from the city, back in the mundane life of the country.

Arredondo also had a chessboard on which he would play chaotic games that never managed to come to any end. A rook was missing; he would use a bullet or a coin in its place.

To pass the time, every morning Arredondo would clean his room with a rag and a big broom, even chasing down spiderwebs. The black woman didn't like him to lower himself to such chores—not only because they fell within her purview but also because Arredondo didn't really do them very well.

He would have liked to wake up when the sun was high, but the habit of getting up with the dawn was stronger than his mere will. He missed his friends terribly, though he knew without bitterness that they didn't miss him, given his impregnable reserve. One afternoon, one of them came around to ask after him but was met in the vestibule and turned away. The black woman didn't know him; Arredondo never learned who it had been. An avid reader of the news, Arredondo found it hard to renounce those museums of ephemera. He was not a thinking man, or one much given to meditation.

His days and his nights were the same, but Sundays weighed on him.

In mid-July he surmised he'd been mistaken in parceling out his time, which bears us along one way or another anyway. At that point he allowed his imagination to wander through the wide countryside of his homeland, now bloody, through the rough fields of Santa Irene where he had once flown kites, to a certain stocky little piebald horse, surely dead by now, through the dust raised by the cattle when the drovers herded them in, to

the exhausted stagecoach that arrived every month with its load
of trinkets from Fray Bentos, through the bay of La Agraciada
where the Thirty-three came ashore, to the Hervidero, through
ragged mountains, wildernesses, and rivers, through the Cerro he
had scaled to the lighthouse, thinking that on the two banks of
the River Plate there was not another like it. From the Cerro on
the bay he traveled once to the peak on the Uruguayan coat of
arms,* and he fell asleep.

Each night the sea breeze was cool, and good for sleeping. He
never spent a sleepless night.

He loved his sweetheart with all his soul, but he'd been told
that a man shouldn't think about women, especially when there
were none to be had. Being in the country had accustomed him
to chastity. As for the other matter . . . he tried to think as little
as possible of the man he hated.

The sound of the rain on the roof was company for him.

For the man in prison, or the blind man, time flows downstream
as though down a slight decline. As he reached the midpoint of
his reclusion, Arredondo more than once achieved that virtually
timeless time. In the first patio there was a wellhead, and at the
bottom, a cistern where a toad lived; it never occurred to Arredondo that it was the toad's time, bordering on eternity, that he
sought.

As the day grew near he began to be impatient again. One
night he couldn't bear it anymore, and he went out for a walk.
Everything seemed different, bigger. As he turned a corner, he
saw a light and went into the general store, where there was a
bar. In order to justify being there, he called for a shot of cane
brandy. Sitting and talking, their elbows on the wooden bar, were
some soldiers. One of them said:

"All of you know that it's strictly outlawed to give out any
news about battles—formal orders against it. Well, yesterday
afternoon something happened to us that you boys are going to
like. Some barracks-mates of mine and I were walking along in

front of the newspaper over there, *La Razón*. And we heard a voice inside that was breaking that order. We didn't waste a second going in there, either. The city room was as dark as pitch, but we gunned down that loose-lipped traitor that was talking. When he finally shut up, we hunted around for him to drag him out by the heels, but we saw it was a machine!—a *phonograph* they call it, and it talks all by itself!"

Everyone laughed.

Arredondo had been listening intently.

"What do you think—pretty disappointing, eh, buddy?"

Arredondo said nothing. The uniformed man put his face very near Arredondo's.

"I want to hear how loud you can yell *Viva the President of our Country, Juan Idiarte Borda!*"*

Arredondo did not disobey. Amid jeers and clapping he gained the door; in the street, he was hit by one last insult:

"Nobody ever said cowards were stupid—or had much temper, either!"

He had behaved like a coward, but he knew he wasn't one. He returned slowly and deliberately to his house.

On August 25, Avelino Arredondo woke up at a little past nine. He thought first of Clara, and only later of what day it was. *Good-bye to all this work of waiting—I've made it*, he said to himself in relief.

He shaved slowly, taking his time, and in the mirror he met the same face as always. He picked out a red tie and his best clothes. He had a late lunch. The gray sky threatened drizzle; he'd always pictured this day as radiant. He felt a touch of bitterness at leaving his damp room forever. In the vestibule he met the black woman, and he gave her the last pesos that were left. On the sign at the hardware store he saw some colored diamond shapes, and he realized it had been more than two months since he'd thought of them. He headed toward Calle Sarandi. It was a holiday, and very few people were about.

It was not yet three o'clock when he reached the Plaza Matriz. The *Te Deum* had been sung; a group of well-dressed men, military officers, and prelates was coming down the slow steps of the church. At first glance, the top hats (some still in their hands), the uniforms, the gold braid, the weapons, and the tunics might create the illusion that there were many of them; the truth was, there were no more than about thirty. Though Arredondo felt no fear, he did feel a kind of respect. He asked which of the men was the president.

"The one there walking beside the archbishop with the miter and staff," he was told.

He took out his pistol and fired.

Idiarte Borda took a few steps, fell forward to the ground, and said very clearly, "I've been killed."

Arredondo gave himself up to the authorities.

"I am a Red and I'm proud to say so. I have killed the president, who betrayed and sullied our party. I left my friends and my sweetheart so they would not be dragged into this; I didn't read the newspapers so that no one could say the newspapers incited me to do this. I alone am responsible for this act of justice. Now try me."

This is how the events* might have taken place, though perhaps in a more complex way; this is how I can dream they happened.

The Disk

I am a woodcutter. My name doesn't matter. The hut I was born in, and where I'm soon to die, sits at the edge of the woods. They say these woods go on and on, right to the ocean that surrounds the entire world; they say that wooden houses like mine travel on that ocean. I wouldn't know; I've never seen it. I've not seen the *other* side of the woods, either. My older brother, when we were boys he made me swear that between the two of us we'd hack away at this woods till there wasn't a tree left standing. My brother is dead now, and now it's something else I'm after, and always will be. Over in the direction where the sun goes down there's a creek I fish in with my hands. There are wolves in the woods, but the wolves don't scare me, and my ax has never failed me. I've not kept track of how old I am, but I know I'm old—my eyes don't see anymore. Down in the village, which I don't venture into anymore because I'd lose my way, everyone says I'm a miser, but how much could a woodcutter have saved up?

I keep the door of my house shut with a rock so the snow won't get in. One evening I heard heavy, dragging footsteps and then a knock. I opened the door and a stranger came in. He was a tall, elderly man all wrapped up in a worn-out old blanket. A scar sliced across his face. The years looked to have given him more authority than frailty, but even so I saw it was hard for him to walk without leaning on his stick. We exchanged a few words I don't recall now. Then finally the man said:

"I am without a home, and I sleep wherever I can. I have wandered all across Saxony."

His words befitted his age. My father always talked about "Saxony"; now people call it England.

There was bread and some fish in the house. While we ate, we didn't talk. It started raining. I took some skins and made him a pallet on the dirt floor where my brother had died. When night came we slept.

It was toward dawn when we left the house. The rain had stopped and the ground was covered with new snow. The man dropped his stick and he ordered me to pick it up.

"Why should I do what you tell me to?" I said to him.

"Because I am a king," he answered.

I thought he was mad. I picked up the stick and gave it to him. With his next words, his voice was changed.

"I am the king of the Secgens. Many times did I lead them to victory in hard combat, but at the hour that fate decreed, I lost my kingdom. My name is Isern and I am of the line of Odin."

"I do not worship Odin," I answered. "I worship Christ."

He went on as though he'd not heard me.

"I wander the paths of exile, but still I am king, for I have the disk. Do you want to see it?"

He opened his hand and showed me his bony palm. There was nothing in it. His hand was empty. It was only then that I realized he'd always kept it shut tight.

He looked me in the eye.

"You may touch it."

I had my doubts, but I reached out and with my fingertips I touched his palm. I felt something cold, and I saw a quick gleam. His hand snapped shut. I said nothing.

"It is the disk of Odin," the old man said in a patient voice, as though he were speaking to a child. "It has but one side. There is not another thing on earth that has but one side. So long as I hold it in my hand I shall be king."

"Is it gold?" I said.

"I know not. It is the disk of Odin and it has but one side."

It was then I felt a gnawing to own the disk myself. If it were mine, I could sell it for a bar of gold and then *I* would be a king.

"In my hut I've got a chest full of money hidden away. Gold coins, and they shine like my ax," I told the wanderer, whom I hate to this day. "If you give the disk of Odin to me, I will give you the chest."

"I will not," he said gruffly.

"Then you can continue on your way," I said.

He turned away. One ax blow to the back of his head was all it took; he wavered and fell, but as he fell he opened his hand, and I saw the gleam of the disk in the air. I marked the place with my ax and I dragged the body down to the creek bed, where I knew the creek was swollen. There I dumped his body.

When I got back to my house I looked for the disk. But I couldn't find it. I have been looking for it for years.

The Book of Sand

... *thy rope of sands* ... George Herbert (1593–1623)

The line consists of an infinite number of points; the plane, of an infinite number of lines; the volume, of an infinite number of planes; the hypervolume, of an infinite number of volumes . . . No—this, *more geometrico*, is decidedly not the best way to begin my tale. To say that the story is true is by now a convention of every fantastic tale; mine, nevertheless, *is* true.

I live alone, in a fifth-floor apartment on Calle Belgrano. One evening a few months ago, I heard a knock at my door. I opened it, and a stranger stepped in. He was a tall man, with blurred, vague features, or perhaps my nearsightedness made me see him that way. Everything about him spoke of honest poverty: he was dressed in gray, and carried a gray valise. I immediately sensed that he was a foreigner. At first I thought he was old; then I noticed that I had been misled by his sparse hair, which was blond, almost white, like the Scandinavians'. In the course of our conversation, which I doubt lasted more than an hour, I learned that he hailed from the Orkneys.

I pointed the man to a chair. He took some time to begin talking. He gave off an air of melancholy, as I myself do now.

"I sell Bibles," he said at last.

"In this house," I replied, not without a somewhat stiff, pedantic note, "there are several English Bibles, including the first one, Wyclif's. I also have Cipriano de Valera's, Luther's (which is, in literary terms, the worst of the lot), and a Latin copy of the Vulgate. As you see, it isn't exactly Bibles I might be needing."

After a brief silence he replied.

"It's not only Bibles I sell. I can show you a sacred book that might interest a man such as yourself. I came by it in northern India, in Bikaner."

He opened his valise and brought out the book. He laid it on the table. It was a clothbound octavo volume that had clearly passed through many hands. I examined it; the unusual heft of it surprised me. On the spine was printed *Holy Writ*, and then *Bombay*.

"Nineteenth century, I'd say," I observed.

"I don't know," was the reply. "Never did know."

I opened it at random. The characters were unfamiliar to me. The pages, which seemed worn and badly set, were printed in double columns, like a Bible. The text was cramped, and composed into versicles. At the upper corner of each page were Arabic numerals. I was struck by an odd fact: the even-numbered page would carry the number 40,514, let us say, while the odd-numbered page that followed it would be 999. I turned the page; the next page bore an eight-digit number. It also bore a small illustration, like those one sees in dictionaries: an anchor drawn in pen and ink, as though by the unskilled hand of a child.

It was at that point that the stranger spoke again.

"Look at it well. You will never see it again."

There was a threat in the words, but not in the voice.

I took note of the page, and then closed the book. Immediately I opened it again. In vain I searched for the figure of the anchor, page after page. To hide my discomfiture, I tried another tack.

"This is a version of Scripture in some Hindu language, isn't that right?"

"No," he replied.

Then he lowered his voice, as though entrusting me with a secret.

"I came across this book in a village on the plain, and I traded a few rupees and a Bible for it. The man who owned it didn't know how to read. I suspect he saw the Book of Books as an amulet. He was of the lowest caste; people could not so much as step on his shadow without being defiled. He told me his book was called the Book of Sand because neither sand nor this book has a beginning or an end."

He suggested I try to find the first page.

I took the cover in my left hand and opened the book, my thumb and forefinger almost touching. It was impossible: several pages always lay between the cover and my hand. It was as though they grew from the very book.

"Now try to find the end."

I failed there as well.

"This can't be," I stammered, my voice hardly recognizable as my own.

"It can't be, yet it *is*," The Bible peddler said, his voice little more than a whisper. "The number of pages in this book is literally infinite. No page is the first page; no page is the last. I don't know why they're numbered in this arbitrary way, but perhaps it's to give one to understand that the terms of an infinite series can be numbered any way whatever."

Then, as though thinking out loud, he went on.

"If space is infinite, we are anywhere, at any point in space. If time is infinite, we are at any point in time."

His musings irritated me.

"You," I said, "are a religious man, are you not?"

"Yes, I'm Presbyterian. My conscience is clear. I am certain I didn't cheat that native when I gave him the Lord's Word in exchange for his diabolic book."

I assured him he had nothing to reproach himself for, and asked whether he was just passing through the country. He replied that he planned to return to his own country within a few days. It was then that I learned he was a Scot, and that his home was in the Orkneys. I told him I had great personal fondness for Scotland because of my love for Stevenson and Hume.

"And Robbie Burns," he corrected.

As we talked I continued to explore the infinite book.

"Had you intended to offer this curious specimen to the British Museum, then?" I asked with feigned indifference.

"No," he replied, "I am offering it to you," and he mentioned a great sum of money.

I told him, with perfect honesty, that such an amount of money was not within my ability to pay. But my mind was working; in a few moments I had devised my plan.

"I propose a trade," I said. "You purchased the volume with a few rupees and the Holy Scripture; I will offer you the full sum of my pension, which I have just received, and Wyclif's black-letter Bible. It was left to me by my parents."

"A black-letter Wyclif!" he murmured.

I went to my bedroom and brought back the money and the book. With a bibliophile's zeal he turned the pages and studied the binding.

"Done," he said.

I was astonished that he did not haggle. Only later was I to realize that he had entered my house already determined to sell the book. He did not count the money, but merely put the bills into his pocket.

We chatted about India, the Orkneys, and the Norwegian jarls that had once ruled those islands. Night was falling when the man left. I have never seen him since, nor do I know his name.

I thought of putting the Book of Sand in the space left by the Wyclif, but I chose at last to hide it behind some imperfect volumes of the *Thousand and One Nights*.

I went to bed but could not sleep. At three or four in the morning I turned on the light. I took out the impossible book and turned its pages. On one, I saw an engraving of a mask. There was a number in the corner of the page—I don't remember now what it was—raised to the ninth power.

I showed no one my treasure. To the joy of possession was added the fear that it would be stolen from me, and to that, the suspicion that it might not be truly infinite. Those two points of anxiety aggravated my already habitual misanthropy. I had but few friends left, and those, I stopped seeing. A prisoner of the Book, I hardly left my house. I examined the worn binding and the covers with a magnifying glass, and rejected the possibility of some artifice. I found that the small illustrations were spaced at two-thousand-page intervals. I began noting them down in an alphabetized notebook, which was very soon filled. They never repeated themselves. At night, during the rare intervals spared me by insomnia, I dreamed of the book.

Summer was drawing to a close, and I realized that the book was monstrous. It was cold consolation to think that I, who looked upon it with my eyes and fondled it with my ten flesh-and-bone fingers, was no less monstrous than the book. I felt it was a nightmare thing, an obscene thing, and that it defiled and corrupted reality.

I considered fire, but I feared that the burning of an infinite book might be similarly infinite, and suffocate the planet in smoke.

I remembered reading once that the best place to hide a leaf is in the forest. Before my retirement I had worked in the National Library, which contained nine hundred thousand books; I knew that to the right of the lobby a curving staircase descended into the shadows of the basement, where the maps and periodicals are kept. I took advantage of the librarians' distraction to hide the Book of Sand on one of the library's damp shelves; I tried not to notice how high up, or how far from the door.

I now feel a little better, but I refuse even to walk down the street the library's on.*

Afterword

Writing a foreword to stories the reader has not yet read is an almost impossible task, for it requires that one talk about plots that really ought not to be revealed beforehand. I have chosen, therefore, to write an afterword instead.

The first story once more takes up the old theme of the double, which so often inspired Stevenson's ever-happy pen. In England the double is called the fetch *or, more literarily,* the wraith of the living; *in Germany it is known as the* Doppelgänger. *I suspect that one of its first aliases was the* alter ego. *This spectral apparition no doubt emerged from mirrors of metal or water, or simply from the memory, which makes each person both spectator and actor. My duty was to ensure that the interlocutors were different enough from each other to be two, yet similar enough to each other to be one. Do you suppose it's worth saying that I conceived the story on the banks of the Charles River, in New England, and that its cold stream reminded me of the distant waters of the Rhône?*

The subject of love is quite common in my poetry; not so in my prose, where the only example is "Ulrikke." Readers will perceive its formal affinity with "The Other."

"The Congress" is perhaps the most ambitious of this book's fables; its subject is a company so vast that it merges at last into the cosmos itself and into the sum of days. The story's murky beginning attempts to imitate the way Kafka's stories begin; its ending attempts, no doubt unsuccessfully, to ascend to the ecstasy of Chesterton or John Bunyan. I have never merited such a revelation, but I have tried to dream of it. In the course of the story I have interwoven, as is my wont, certain autobiographical features.

Fate, which is widely known to be inscrutable, would not leave me in peace until I had perpetrated a posthumous story by Lovecraft, a writer I have always considered an unwitting parodist of Poe. At last I gave in; the lamentable result is titled "There Are More Things."

"The Sect of the Thirty" saves from oblivion (without the slightest documentary support) the history of a possible heresy.

"The Night of the Gifts" is perhaps the most innocent, violent, and overwrought of these tales.

"The Library of Babel," written in 1941, envisions an infinite number of books; "'Undr'" and "The Mirror and the Mask" envision age-old literatures consisting of but a single word.

"A Weary Man's Utopia" is, in my view, the most honest, and most melancholy, piece in the book.

I have always been surprised by the Americans' obsession with ethics; "The Bribe" is an attempt to portray that trait.

In spite of John Felton, Charlotte Corday, and the well-known words of Rivera Indarte ("It is a holy deed to kill Rosas") and the Uruguayan national anthem ("For tyrants, Brutus' blade"), I do not approve of political assassination. Be that as it may, readers of the story of Arredondo's solitary crime will want to know its dénouement. *Luis Melián Lafinur asked that he be pardoned, but Carlos Fein and Cristóbal Salvañac, the judges, sentenced him to one month in solitary confinement and five years in prison. A street in Montevideo now bears his name.*

Two unlucky and inconceivable objects are the subject of the last two stories. "The Disk" is the Euclidean circle, which has but one face; "The Book of Sand," a volume of innumerable pages.

I doubt that the hurried notes I have just dictated will exhaust this book, but hope, rather, that the dreams herein will continue to ramify within the hospitable imaginations of the readers who now close it.

J.L.B.
Buenos Aires, February 3, 1975

Shakespeare's Memory
(1983)

August 25, 1983

I saw by the clock at the little station that it was past eleven. I began walking through the night toward the hotel. I experienced, as I had at other times in the past, the resignation and relief we are made to feel by those places most familiar to us. The wide gate was open; the large country house itself, in darkness. I went into the vestibule, whose pale mirrors echoed back the plants of the salon. Strangely, the owner did not recognize me; he turned the guest register around for me to sign. I picked up the pen chained to the register stand, dipped it in the brass inkwell, and then, as I leaned over the open book, there occurred the first of the many surprises the night would have in store for me——my name, Jorge Luis Borges, had already been written there, and the ink was not yet dry.

"I thought you'd already gone upstairs," the owner said to me. Then he looked at me more closely and corrected himself: "Oh, I beg your pardon, sir. You look so much like the other gentleman, but you are younger."

"What room is he in?" I asked.

"He asked for Room 19," came the reply.

It was as I had feared.

I dropped the pen and hurried up the stairs. Room 19 was on the third floor; it opened onto a sad, run-down sort of terrace with a park bench and, as I recall, a railing running around it. It was the hotel's most secluded room. I tried the door; it opened at my touch. The overhead light still burned. In the pitiless light, I came face to face with myself. There, in the narrow iron bed—older, withered, and very pale—lay I, on my back, my eyes turned up vacantly toward the high plaster moldings of the ceiling. Then I heard the voice. It was not exactly my own; it was the one I often hear in my recordings, unpleasant and without modulation.

"How odd," it was saying, "we are two yet we are one. But then nothing is odd in dreams."

"Then . . ." I asked fearfully, "all this is a dream?"

"It is, I am sure, my last dream." He gestured toward the empty bottle on the marble nightstand. "You, however, shall have much to dream, before you come to this night. What date is it for you?"

"I'm not sure," I said, rattled. "But yesterday was my sixty-first birthday."

"When in your waking state you reach this night again, yesterday will have been your eighty-fourth. Today is August 25, 1983."

"So long to wait," I murmured.

"Not for me," he said shortly. "For me, there's almost no time left. At any moment I may die, at any moment I may fade into that which is unknown to me, and still I dream these dreams of my double . . . that tiresome subject I got from Stevenson and mirrors."

I sensed that the evocation of Stevenson's name was a farewell, not some empty stroke of pedantry. I was he, and I understood. It takes more than life's most dramatic moments to make a Shakespeare, hitting upon memorable phrases. To distract him, I said:

"I knew this was going to happen to you. Right here in this hotel, years ago, in one of the rooms below, we began the draft of the story of this suicide."

"Yes," he replied slowly, as though piecing together the memories, "but I don't see the connection. In that draft I bought a one-way ticket for Adrogué,* and when I got to the Hotel Las Delicias I went up to Room 19, the room farthest from all the rest. It was there that I committed suicide."

"That's why I'm here," I said.

"*Here?* We've always been *here*. It's here in this house on Calle Maipú that I am dreaming you. It is here, in this room that belonged to Mother, that I am taking my departure."

". . . that belonged to Mother," I repeated, not wanting to understand. "I am dreaming you in Room 19, on the top floor, next to the rooftop terrace."

"Who is dreaming whom? I know I am dreaming you—I do not know whether you are dreaming me. That hotel in Adrogué was torn down years and years ago—twenty, maybe thirty. Who knows?"

"I am the dreamer," I replied, with a touch of defiance.

"Don't you realize that the first thing to find out is whether there is only one man dreaming, or two men dreaming each other?"

"I am Borges. I saw your name in the register and I came upstairs."

"But I am Borges, and I am dying in a house on Calle Maipú."

There was a silence, and then he said to me:

"Let's try a test. What was the most terrible moment of our life?"

I leaned over him and the two of us spoke at once. I know that neither of us spoke the truth.

A faint smile lit up the aged face. I felt that that smile somehow reflected my own.

"We've lied to each other," he said, "because we feel that we are two, not one. The truth is that we are two yet we are one."

I was beginning to be irritated by this conversation, and I told him so. Then I added: "And you, there in 1983—are you not going to tell me anything about the years I have left?"

"What can I tell you, poor Borges? The misfortunes you are already accustomed to will repeat themselves. You will be left alone in this house. You will touch the books that have no letters and the Swedenborg medallion and the wooden tray with the

Federal Cross. Blindness is not darkness; it is a form of solitude. You will return to Iceland."

"Iceland! Sea-girt Iceland!"

"In Rome, you will once more recite the poetry of Keats, whose name, like all men's names, was writ in water."

"I've never been in Rome."

"There are other things. You will write our best poem—an elegy."

"On the death of . . ." I began. I could not bring myself to say the name.

"No. She will outlive *you.*"

We grew silent. Then he went on:

"You will write the book we've dreamed of for so long. In 1979 you will see that your supposed career has been nothing but a series of drafts, miscellaneous drafts, and you will give in to the vain and superstitious temptation to write your great book—the superstition that inflicted upon us Goethe's *Faust*, and *Salammbô*, and *Ulysses*. I filled, incredible to tell, many, many pages."

"And in the end you realized that you had failed."

"Worse. I realized that it was a masterpiece in the most overwhelming sense of the word. My good intentions hadn't lasted beyond the first pages; those that followed held the labyrinths, the knives, the man who thinks he's an image, the reflection that thinks it's real, the tiger that stalks in the night, the battles that are in one's blood, the blind and fatal Juan Muraña, the voice of Macedonio Fernández, the ship made with the fingernails of the dead, Old English repeated in the evening."

"That museum rings a bell," I remarked sarcastically.

"Not to mention false recollections, the doubleness of symbols, the long catalogs, the skilled handling of prosaic reality, the imperfect symmetries that critics so jubilantly discover, the not always apocryphal quotations."

"Did you publish it?"

"I toyed, without conviction, with the melodramatic possibility of destroying the book, perhaps by fire. But I wound up publishing it in Madrid, under a pseudonym. I was taken for a clumsy imitator of Borges—a person who had the defect of not actually being Borges yet of mirroring all the outward appearances of the original."

"I'm not surprised," I said. "Every writer sooner or later becomes his own least intelligent disciple."

"That book was one of the roads that led me to this night. The others . . . The humiliation of old age, the conviction of having already lived each day . . ."

"I will not write that book," I said.

"You will, though. My words, which are now your present, will one day be but the vaguest memory of a dream."

I found myself annoyed by his dogmatic tone, the tone that I myself no doubt use in my classes. I was annoyed by the fact that we resembled each other so much and that he was taking advantage of the impunity lent him by the nearness of death.

"Are you so sure," I said, to get back at him a bit, "that you're going to die?"

"Yes," he replied. "I feel a sort of sweetness and relief I've never felt before. I can't describe it; all words require a shared experience. Why do you seem so annoyed at what I'm saying?"

"Because we're too much like each other. I loathe your face, which is a caricature of mine, I loathe your voice, which is a mockery of mine, I loathe your pathetic syntax, which is my own."

"So do I," he smiled. "Which is why I decided to kill myself."

A bird sang from the garden.

"It's the last one," the other man said.

He motioned me toward him. His hand sought mine. I stepped back; I was afraid the two hands would merge.

"The Stoics teach," he said to me, "that we should not complain of life—the door of the prison is open. I have always understood that; I myself saw life that way, but laziness and cowardice held me back. About twelve days ago, I was giving a lecture in La Plata on Book VI of the *Æneid*. Suddenly, as I was scanning a hexameter, I discovered what my path was to be. I made this decision—and since that moment, I have felt myself invulnerable. You shall one day meet that fate—you shall receive that sudden revelation, in the midst of Latin and Virgil, yet you will have utterly forgotten this curious prophetic dialogue that is taking place in two times and two places. When you next dream it, you shall be who I am, and you shall be my dream."

"I won't forget it—I'm going to write it down tomorrow."

"It will lie in the depths of your memory, beneath the tides of your dreams. When you write it, you will think that you're weaving a tale of fantasy. And it won't be tomorrow, either—it will be many years from now."

He stopped talking; I realized that he had died. In a way, I died with him—in grief I leaned over his pillow, but there was no one there anymore.

I fled the room. Outside, there was no patio, no marble staircase, no great silent house, no eucalyptus trees, no statues, no gazebo in a garden, no fountains, no gate in the fence surrounding the hotel in the town of Adrogué.

Outside awaited other dreams.

Blue Tigers

A famous poem by Blake paints the tiger as a fire burning bright and an eternal archetype of Evil; I prefer the Chesterton maxim that casts the tiger as a symbol of terrible elegance. Apart from these, there are no words that can rune the tiger, that shape which for centuries has lived in the imagination of mankind. I have always been drawn to the tiger. I know that as a boy I would linger before one particular cage at the zoo; the others held no interest for me. I would judge encyclopedias and natural histories by their engravings of the tiger. When the *Jungle Books* were revealed to me I was upset that the tiger, Shere Khan, was the hero's enemy. As the years passed, this strange fascination never left me; it survived my paradoxical desire to become a hunter as it did all common human vicissitudes. Until not long ago (the date feels distant but it really is not), it coexisted peacefully with my day-to-day labors at the University of Lahore. I am a professor of Eastern and Western logic, and I consecrate my Sundays to a seminar on the philosophy of Spinoza. I should add that I am a Scotsman; it may have been my love of tigers that brought me from Aberdeen to Punjab. The outward course of my life has been the common one, but in my dreams I always saw tigers. Now it is other forms that fill them.

I have recounted all these facts more than once, until now they seem almost to belong to someone else. I let them stand, however, since they are required by my statement.

★

Toward the end of 1904, I read that in the region of the Ganges delta a blue variety of the species had been discovered. The news was confirmed by subsequent telegrams, with the contradictions and incongruities that one expects in such cases. My old love stirred once more. Nevertheless, I suspected some error, since the names of colors are notoriously imprecise. I remembered having once read that in Icelandic, Ethiopia was "Blaland," Blue Land *or* the Land of Black Men. The blue tiger might well be a black panther. Nothing was mentioned of stripes; the picture published by the London press, showing a blue tiger with silver stripes, was patently apocryphal. Similarly, the blue of the illustration looked more like that of heraldry than reality. In a dream, I saw tigers of a blue I had never seen before, and for which I could find no word. I know it was almost black, but that description of course does scant justice to the shade I saw.

Some months later, a colleague of mine told me that in a certain village miles from the Ganges he had heard talk of blue tigers. I was astonished by that piece of news, because tigers are rare in that area. Once again I dreamed of the blue tiger, throwing its long shadow as it made its way over the sandy ground. I took advantage of the end of term to make a journey to that village, whose name (for reasons that will soon be clear) I do not wish to recall.

I arrived toward the end of the rainy season. The village squatted at the foot of a hill (which looked to me wider than it was high) and was surrounded and menaced by the jungle, which was a dark brown color. Surely one of the pages of Kipling contains that village of my adventure, since all of India, all the world somehow, can be found there. Suffice it to report that a ditch, and swaying cane-stalk bridges, constituted the huts' fragile defense. Toward the south there were swamps and rice fields and a ravine with a muddy river whose name I never learned, and beyond that, again, the jungle.

The people who lived in the village were Hindus. I did not

Blue Tigers

like this, though I had foreseen it. I have always gotten along better with Muslims, though Islam, I know, is the poorest of the religions that spring from Judaism.

We feel ordinarily that India teems with humanity; in the village I felt that India teemed with *jungle.* It crept virtually into the huts. The days were oppressive, and the nights brought no relief.

I was greeted upon my arrival by the elders, with whom I sustained a tentative conversation constructed of vague courtesies. I have mentioned the poverty of the place, but I know that it is an axiom of every man's belief that the land he lives in and owes his allegiance to possesses some unique distinction, and so I praised in glowing terms the dubious habitations and the no less dubious delicacies served me, and I declared that the fame of that region had reached Lahore. The expressions on the men's faces changed; I immediately sensed that I had committed a *faux pas* I might come to regret. I sensed that these people possessed a secret they would not share with a stranger. Perhaps they worshiped the blue tiger, perhaps they were devotees of a cult that my rash words had profaned.

I waited until the next morning. When the rice had been consumed and the tea drunk down, I broached my subject. Despite the previous night's experience, I did not understand—was incapable of understanding—what took place then. The entire village looked at me with stupefaction, almost with terror, but when I told them that my purpose was to capture the beast with the curious skin, they seemed almost relieved at my words. One of them said he had seen the animal at the edge of the jungle.

In the middle of the night, they woke me. A boy told me that a goat had escaped from the corral and that as he'd gone to look for it, he'd seen the blue tiger on the far bank of the river. I reflected that the scant light of the new moon would hardly have allowed him to make out the color, but everyone confirmed the tale; one of them, who had been silent up until that moment, said he had seen it, too. We went out with the rifles and I saw, or thought I saw, a feline shadow slink into the shadows of the jungle. They did not find the goat, but the creature that had taken it might or might not have been my blue tiger. They emphatically pointed out to me other traces—which of course proved nothing.

After a few nights I realized that these false alarms were a sort of routine. Like Daniel Defoe, the men of the village were skilled at inventing circumstantial details. The tiger might be glimpsed at any hour, out toward the rice fields to the south or up toward the jungle to the north, but it did not take me long to realize that there was a suspicious regularity in the way the villagers seemed to take turns spotting it. My arrival upon the scene of the sighting invariably coincided with the precise instant that the tiger had just run off. I was always shown a trail, a paw mark, some broken twig, but a man's fist can counterfeit a tiger's prints. Once or twice I witnessed a dead dog. One moonlit night we staked out a goat as a lure, but we watched fruitlessly until dawn. I thought at first that these daily fables were meant to encourage me to prolong my stay, for it did benefit the village—the people sold me food and did domestic chores for me. To verify this conjecture, I told them that I was thinking of moving on to another region, downstream, in quest of the tiger. I was surprised to find that they welcomed my decision. I continued to sense, however, that there was a secret, and that everyone was keeping a wary eye on me.

I mentioned earlier that the wooded hill at whose foot the village sprawled was not really very high; it was flat on top, a sort of plateau. On the other side of the mountain, toward the west and north, the jungle began again. Since the slope was not a rugged one, one afternoon I suggested that we climb it. My simple words threw the villagers into consternation. One exclaimed that the mountainside was too steep. The eldest of them said gravely that my goal was impossible to attain, the summit of the hill was sacred, magical obstacles blocked the ascent to man. He who trod the peak with mortal foot was in danger of seeing the godhead, and of going blind or mad.

I did not argue, but that night, when everyone was asleep, I stole soundlessly from my hut and began to climb the easy hillside.

There was no path, and the undergrowth held me back. The moon was just at the horizon. I took note of everything with singular attentiveness, as though I sensed that this was to be an important day, perhaps the most important day of all my days. I still recall the dark, almost black, shadings of the leaves and bushes. It was close to dawn, and the sky was beginning to turn pale, but in all the jungle around, not one bird sang.

Twenty or thirty minutes' climb brought me to the summit. It took me very little effort to imagine that it was cooler there than in the village, which sweltered down below. I had been right that this was not a peak, but rather a plateau, a sort of terrace, not very broad, and that the jungle crept up to it all around, on the flanks of the hill. I felt free, as though my residence in the village had been a prison. I didn't care that the villagers had tried to fool me; I felt they were somehow children.

As for the tiger ... Constant frustration had exhausted my curiosity and my faith, but almost mechanically I looked for tracks.

The ground was cracked and sandy. In one of the cracks— which by the way were not deep, and which branched into others—I caught a glimpse of a color. Incredibly, it was the same color as the tiger of my dreams. I wish I had never laid eyes on it. I looked closely. The crevice was full of little stones, all alike, circular, just a few centimeters in diameter and very smooth. Their regularity lent them an air almost of artificiality, as though they were coins, or buttons, or counters in some game.

I bent down, put my hand into the crevice, and picked out some of the stones. I felt a faint quivering. I put the handful of little stones in the right pocket of my jacket, where there were a small pair of scissors and a letter from Allahabad. Those two chance objects have their place in my story.

Back in my hut, I took off my jacket. I lay down and dreamed once more of the tiger. In my dream I took special note of its color; it was the color of the tiger I had dreamed of, and also of the little stones from the plateau. The late-morning sun in my face woke me. I got up. The scissors and the letter made it hard to take the disks out of the pocket; they kept getting in the way. I pulled out a handful, but felt that there were still two or three I had missed. A tickling sensation, the slightest sort of quivering, imparted a soft warmth to my palm. When I opened my hand, I saw that it held thirty or forty disks; I'd have sworn I'd picked up no more than ten. I left them on the table and turned back to get the rest out of the pocket. I didn't need to count them to see that they had multiplied. I pushed them together into a single pile, and tried to count them out one by one.

That simple operation turned out to be impossible. I would look fixedly at any one of them, pick it up with my thumb and index finger, yet when I had done that, when that one disk was separated from the rest, it would have become many. I checked to see that I didn't have a fever (which I did not), and then I performed the same experiment, over and over again. The obscene miracle kept happening. I felt my feet go clammy and my bowels turn to ice; my knees began to shake. I do not know how much time passed.

Without looking at the disks, I scooped them into a pile and threw them out the window. With a strange feeling of relief, I sensed that their number had dwindled. I firmly closed the door and lay down on my bed. I tried to find the exact position I had been lying in before, hoping to persuade myself that all this had been a dream. So as not to think about the disks yet somehow fill the time, I repeated, with slow precision, aloud, the eight definitions and seven axioms of Ethics. I am not sure they helped.

In the midst of these exorcistic exercises, a knock came at my door. Instinctively fearing that I had been overheard talking to myself, I went to the door and opened it.

It was the headman of the village, Bhagwan Dass. For a second his presence seemed to restore me to everyday reality. We stepped outside. I harbored some hope that the disks might have disappeared, but there they were, on the ground. I no longer can be sure how many there were.

The elder looked down at them and then looked at me.

"These stones are not from here. They are stones from up there," he said, in a voice that was not his own.

"That's true," I replied. I added, not without some defiance, that I had found them up on the plateau, but I was immediately ashamed of myself for feeling that I owed anyone an explanation. Bhagwan Dass ignored me; he continued to stare in fascination at the stones. I ordered him to pick them up. He did not move.

I am grieved to admit that I took out my revolver and repeated the order, this time in a somewhat more forceful tone of voice.

"A bullet in the breast is preferable to a blue stone in the hand," stammered Bhagwan Dass.

"You are a coward," said I.

I was, I believe, no less terrified than he, but I closed my eyes and picked up a handful of stones with my left hand. I tucked the pistol in my belt and dropped the stones one by one into the open palm of my right hand. Their number had grown considerably.

I had unwittingly become accustomed to those transformations. They now surprised me less than Bhagwan Dass' cries.

"These are the stones that spawn!" he exclaimed. "There are many of them now, but they can change. Their shape is that of the moon when it is full, and their color is the blue that we are permitted to see only in our dreams. My father's father spoke the truth when he told men of their power."

The entire village crowded around us.

I felt myself to be the magical possessor of those wondrous objects. To the astonishment of all, I picked up the disks, raised them high, dropped them, scattered them, watched them grow and multiply or mysteriously dwindle.

The villagers huddled together, seized with astonishment and horror. Men forced their wives to look upon the wonder. One woman covered her face with her forearm, another squeezed her eyes shut tight. No one had the courage to touch the disks—save one happy boy-child that played with them. Just at that moment I sensed that all this confusion was profaning the miracle. I gathered the disks, all of them I could, and returned to my hut.

It may be that I have tried to forget the rest of that day, which was the first of a misfortunate series that continues even until now. Whether I tried to forget the day or not, I do not remember it. Toward evening, I began to think back on the night before, which had not been a particularly happy one, with a sort of nostalgia; at least it, like so many others, had been filled with my obsession with the tiger. I tried to find solace in that image once charged with power, now trivial. The blue tiger seemed no less innocuous than the Roman's black swan, which was discovered subsequently in Australia.

Rereading what I have written, I see that I have committed a fundamental error. Led astray by the habit of that good or bad literature wrongly called psychology, I have attempted to recover—I don't know why—the linear chronology of my find. Instead, I should have stressed the monstrousness of the disks.

If someone were to tell me that there are unicorns on the moon, I could accept or reject the report, or suspend judgment, but it is something I could imagine. If, on the other hand, I were told that six or seven unicorns on the moon could be three, I would declare *a priori* that such a thing was impossible. The man who has learned that three plus one are four doesn't have to go through a proof of that assertion with coins, or dice, or chess pieces, or pencils. He knows it, and that's that. He cannot conceive a different sum. There are mathematicians who say that three plus one is a *tautology* for four, a *different way of saying* "four" . . . But I, Alexander Craigie, of all men on earth, was fated to discover the only objects that contradict that essential law of the human mind.

At first I was in a sort of agony, fearing that I'd gone mad;

since then, I have come to believe that it would have been better had I been merely insane, for my personal hallucinations would be less disturbing than the discovery that the universe can tolerate disorder. If three plus one can be two, or fourteen, then reason is madness.

During that time, I often dreamed about the stones. The fact that the dream did not recur every night left me a sliver of hope, though a hope that soon turned to terror. The dream was always more or less the same; the beginning heralded the feared end. A spiral staircase—an iron railing and a few iron treads—and then a cellar, or system of cellars, leading through the depths to other stairways that might abruptly end, or suddenly lead into ironworks, locksmith's forges, dungeons, or swamps. At the bottom, in their expected crevice in the earth, the stones, which were also Behemoth, or Leviathan—the creatures of the Scriptures that signify that God is irrational. I would awaken trembling, and there the stones would be, in their box, ready to transform themselves.

The villagers' attitude toward me began to change. I had been touched by something of the divinity that inhered in the stones the villagers had named "blue tigers," but I was also known to have profaned the summit. At any moment of the night, at any moment of the day, the gods might punish me. The villagers dared not attack me or condemn what I had done, but I noticed that everyone was now dangerously servile. I never again laid eyes on the child who had played with the stones. I feared poison, or a knife in the back. One morning before dawn I slipped out of the village. I sensed that its entire population had been keeping an eye on me, and that my escape would be a relief to them. Since that first morning, no one had ever asked to see the stones.

I returned to Lahore, the handful of disks in my pocket. The familiar environment of my books did not bring the relief I sought. That abominable village, and the jungle, and the jungle's thorny slope rising to the plateau, and on the plateau the little crevices, and within the crevices, the stones—all that, I felt, continued to exist on the planet. My dreams confused and multiplied those dissimilar things. The village was the stones, the jungle was the swamp, the swamp was the jungle.

I shunned the company of my friends. I feared that I would yield to the temptation of showing them that dreadful miracle that undermined humanity's science.

I performed several experiments. I made a cross-shaped incision in one of the disks, put that disk with the others, and shuffled them around; within one or two conversions, I had lost it, though the number of disks had increased. I performed an analogous test with a disk from which I filed a semicircular notch. That disk also disappeared. I punched a hole in the center of one disk with an awl and tried the test again. That disk disappeared forever. The next day the disk with the cross cut in it reappeared from its journey into the void. What mysterious sort of space was this, which in obedience to inscrutable laws or some inhuman will absorbed the stones and then in time threw an occasional one back again?

The same yearning for order that had created mathematics in the first place made me seek some order in that aberration of mathematics, the insensate stones that propagate themselves. I attempted to find a law within their unpredictable variations. I devoted days and nights alike to establishing statistics on the changes. From that stage of my investigations I still have several notebooks, vainly filled with ciphers. My procedure was this: I would count the stones by eye and write down the figure. Then I would divide them into two handfuls that I would scatter separately on the table. I would count the two totals, note them down, and repeat the operation. This search for order, for a secret design within the rotations, led nowhere. The largest number of stones I counted was 419; the smallest, three. There was a moment when I hoped, or feared, that they would disappear altogether. It took little experimenting to show that one of the disks, isolated from the others, could not multiply or disappear.

Naturally, the four mathematical operations—adding, subtracting, multiplying, and dividing—were impossible. The stones resisted arithmetic as they did the calculation of probability. Forty disks, divided, might become nine; those nine in turn divided might yield three hundred. I do not know how much they weighed. I did not have recourse to a scale, but I am sure that their weight was constant, and light. Their color was always that same blue.

These operations helped save me from madness. As I manipulated the stones that destroyed the science of mathematics, more than once I thought of those Greek stones that were the first ciphers and that had been passed down to so many languages as the word "calculus." Mathematics, I told myself, had its origin, and now has its end, in stones. If Pythagoras had worked with these . . .

After about a month I realized that there was no way out of the chaos. There lay the unruly disks, there lay the constant temptation to touch them, to feel that tickling sensation once more, to scatter them, to watch them increase or decrease, and to note whether they came out odd or even. I came to fear that they would contaminate other things—particularly the fingers that insisted upon handling them.

For several days I imposed upon myself the private obligation to think continually about the stones, because I knew that forgetting them was possible only for a moment, and that rediscovering my torment would be unbearable.

I did not sleep the night of February 10. After a walk that led me far into the dawn, I passed through the gates of the mosque of Wazil Khan. It was the hour at which light has not yet revealed the colors of things. There was not a soul in the courtyard. Not knowing why, I plunged my hands into the water of the fountain of ablutions. Inside the mosque, it occurred to me that God and Allah are two names for a single, inconceivable Being, and I prayed aloud that I be freed from my burden. Unmoving, I awaited some reply.

I heard no steps, but a voice, quite close, spoke to me:

"I am here."

A beggar was standing beside me. In the soft light I could make out his turban, his sightless eyes, his sallow skin, his gray beard. He was not very tall.

He put out a hand to me, and said, still softly:

"Alms, oh Protector of the Poor . . ."

I put my hands in my pockets.

"I have not a single coin," I replied.

"You have many," was the beggar's answer.

The stones were in my right pocket. I took out one and dropped it into his cupped palm. There was not the slightest sound.

"You must give me all of them," he said. "He who gives not all has given nothing."

I understood, and I said:

"I want you to know that my alms may be a curse."

"Perhaps that gift is the only gift I am permitted to receive. I have sinned."

I dropped all the stones into the concave hand. They fell as though into the bottom of the sea, without the slightest whisper.

Then the man spoke again:

"I do not yet know what your gift to me is, but mine to you is an awesome one. You may keep your days and nights, and keep wisdom, habits, the world."

I did not hear the blind beggar's steps, or see him disappear into the dawn.

The Rose of Paracelsus

De Quincey: Writings, *XIII,* 345*

Down in his laboratory, to which the two rooms of the cellar had been given over, Paracelsus prayed to his God, his indeterminate God—any God—to send him a disciple.

Night was coming on. The guttering fire in the hearth threw irregular shadows into the room. Getting up to light the iron lamp was too much trouble. Paracelsus, weary from the day, grew absent, and the prayer was forgotten. Night had expunged the dusty retorts and the furnace when there came a knock at his door. Sleepily he got up, climbed the short spiral staircase, and opened one side of the double door. A stranger stepped inside. He too was very tired. Paracelsus gestured toward a bench; the other man sat down and waited. For a while, neither spoke.

The master was the first to speak.

"I recall faces from the West and faces from the East," he said, not without a certain formality, "yet yours I do not recall. Who are you, and what do you wish of me?"

"My name is of small concern," the other man replied. "I have journeyed three days and three nights to come into your house. I wish to become your disciple. I bring you all my possessions."

He brought forth a pouch and emptied its contents on the table. The coins were many, and they were of gold. He did this with his right hand. Paracelsus turned his back to light the lamp;

when he turned around again, he saw that the man's left hand held a rose. The rose troubled him.

He leaned back, put the tips of his fingers together, and said:

"You think that I am capable of extracting the stone that turns all elements to gold, and yet you bring me gold. But it is not gold I seek, and if it is gold that interests you, you shall never be my disciple."

"Gold is of no interest to me," the other man replied. "These coins merely symbolize my desire to join you in your work. I want you to teach me the Art. I want to walk beside you on that path that leads to the Stone."

"The path *is* the Stone. The point of departure is the Stone. If these words are unclear to you, you have not yet begun to understand. Every step you take is the goal you seek." Paracelsus spoke the words slowly.

The other man looked at him with misgiving.

"But," he said, his voice changed, "is there, then, no goal?"

Paracelsus laughed.

"My detractors, who are no less numerous than imbecilic, say that there is not, and they call me an impostor. I believe they are mistaken, though it is possible that I am deluded. I know that there *is* a Path."

There was silence, and then the other man spoke.

"I am ready to walk that Path with you, even if we must walk for many years. Allow me to cross the desert. Allow me to glimpse, even from afar, the promised land, though the stars prevent me from setting foot upon it. All I ask is a proof before we begin the journey."

"When?" said Paracelsus uneasily.

"Now," said the disciple with brusque decisiveness.

They had begun their discourse in Latin; they now were speaking German.

The young man raised the rose into the air.

"You are famed," he said, "for being able to burn a rose to

ashes and make it emerge again, by the magic of your art. Let me witness that prodigy. I ask that of you, and in return I will offer up my entire life."

"You are credulous," the master said. "I have no need of credulity; I demand belief."

The other man persisted.

"It is precisely because I am *not* credulous that I wish to see with my own eyes the annihilation and resurrection of the rose."

"You are credulous," he repeated. "You say that I can destroy it?"

"Any man has the power to destroy it," said the disciple.

"You are wrong," the master responded. "Do you truly believe that something may be turned to nothing? Do you believe that the first Adam in paradise was able to destroy a single flower, a single blade of grass?"

"We are not in paradise," the young man stubbornly replied. "Here, in the sublunary world, all things are mortal."

Paracelsus had risen to his feet.

"Where are we, then, if not in paradise?" he asked. "Do you believe that the deity is able to create a place that is not paradise? Do you believe that the Fall is something other than not realizing that we are in paradise?"

"A rose can be burned," the disciple said defiantly.

"There is still some fire there," said Paracelsus, pointing toward the hearth. "If you cast this rose into the embers, you would believe that it has been consumed, and that its ashes are real. I tell you that the rose is eternal, and that only its appearances may change. At a word from me, you would see it again."

"A word?" the disciple asked, puzzled. "The furnace is cold, and the retorts are covered with dust. What is it you would do to bring it back again?"

Paracelsus looked at him with sadness in his eyes.

"The furnace is cold," he nodded, "and the retorts are covered with dust. On this leg of my long journey I use other instruments."

"I dare not ask what they are," said the other man humbly, or astutely.

"I am speaking of that instrument used by the deity to create the heavens and the earth and the invisible paradise in which we exist, but which original sin hides from us. I am speaking of the Word, which is taught to us by the science of the Kabbalah."

"I ask you," the disciple coldly said, "if you might be so kind as to show me the disappearance and appearance of the rose. It matters not the slightest to me whether you work with alembics or with the Word."

Paracelsus studied for a moment; then he spoke:

"If I did what you ask, you would say that it was an appearance cast by magic upon your eyes. The miracle would not bring you the belief you seek. Put aside, then, the rose."

The young man looked at him, still suspicious. Then Paracelsus raised his voice.

"And besides, who are you to come into the house of a master and demand a miracle of him? What have you done to deserve such a gift?"

The other man, trembling, replied:

"I know I have done nothing. It is for the sake of the many years I will study in your shadow that I ask it of you—allow me to see the ashes and then the rose. I will ask nothing more. I will believe the witness of my eyes."

He snatched up the incarnate and incarnadine rose that Paracelsus had left lying on the table, and he threw it into the flames. Its color vanished, and all that remained was a pinch of ash. For one infinite moment, he awaited the words, and the miracle.

Paracelsus sat unmoving. He said with strange simplicity:

"All the physicians and all the pharmacists in Basel say I am a fraud. Perhaps they are right. There are the ashes that were the rose, and that shall be the rose no more."

The young man was ashamed. Paracelsus was a charlatan, or a mere visionary, and he, an intruder, had come through his door and forced him now to confess that his famed magic arts were false.

He knelt before the master and said:

"What I have done is unpardonable. I have lacked belief, which the Lord demands of all the faithful. Let me, then, continue to see ashes. I will come back again when I am stronger, and I will be your disciple, and at the end of the Path I will see the rose."

He spoke with genuine passion, but that passion was the pity he felt for the agèd master—so venerated, so inveighed against, so renowned, and therefore so hollow. Who was he, Johannes Grisebach, to discover with sacrilegious hand that behind the mask was no one?

Leaving the gold coins would be an act of almsgiving to the poor. He picked them up again as he went out. Paracelsus accompanied him to the foot of the staircase and told him he would always be welcome in that house. Both men knew they would never see each other again.

Paracelsus was then alone. Before putting out the lamp and returning to his weary chair, he poured the delicate fistful of ashes from one hand into the concave other, and he whispered a single word. The rose appeared again.

Shakespeare's Memory

There are devotees of Goethe, of the Eddas, of the late song of the Nibelungen; my fate has been Shakespeare. As it still is, though in a way that no one could have foreseen—no one save one man, Daniel Thorpe, who has just recently died in Pretoria. There is another man, too, whose face I have never seen.

My name is Hermann Sörgel. The curious reader may have chanced to leaf through my *Shakespeare Chronology*, which I once considered essential to a proper understanding of the text: it was translated into several languages, including Spanish. Nor is it beyond the realm of possibility that the reader will recall a protracted diatribe against an emendation inserted by Theobald into his critical edition of 1734—an emendation which became from that moment on an unquestioned part of the canon. Today I am taken a bit aback by the uncivil tone of those pages, which I might almost say were written by another man. In 1914 I drafted, but did not publish, an article on the compound words that the Hellenist and dramatist George Chapman coined for his versions of Homer; in forging these terms, Chapman did not realize that he had carried English back to its Anglo-Saxon origins, the *Ursprung* of the language. It never occurred to me that Chapman's voice, which I have now forgotten, might one day be so familiar to me. . . . A scattering of critical and philological "notes," as they are called, signed with my initials, complete, I believe, my literary biography. Although perhaps I might also be permitted to include an unpublished translation of *Macbeth*, which I began in order to distract my mind from the thought of the death of my brother, Otto Julius, who fell on the western front in 1917. I never finished translating the play; I came to realize that English has (to its credit) two registers—the Germanic and the Latinate—while our own German, in spite of its greater musicality, must content itself with one.

I mentioned Daniel Thorpe. I was introduced to Thorpe by Major Barclay at a Shakespeare conference. I will not say where or when; I know all too well that such specifics are in fact vaguenesses.

More important than Daniel Thorpe's face, which my partial blindness helps me to forget, was his notorious lucklessness. When a man reaches a certain age, there are many things he can feign; happiness is not one of them. Daniel Thorpe gave off an almost physical air of melancholy.

After a long session, night found us in a pub—an undistinguished place that might have been any pub in London. To make ourselves feel that we were in England (which of course we were), we drained many a ritual pewter mug of dark warm beer.

"In Punjab," said the major in the course of our conversation, "a fellow once pointed out a beggar to me. Islamic legend apparently has it, you know, that King Solomon owned a ring that allowed him to understand the language of the birds. And this beggar, so everyone believed, had somehow come into possession of that ring. The value of the thing was so beyond all reckoning that the poor bugger could never sell it, and he died in one of the courtyards of the mosque of Wazil Khan, in Lahore."

It occurred to me that Chaucer must have been familiar with the tale of that miraculous ring, but mentioning it would have spoiled Barclay's anecdote.

"And what became of the ring?" I asked.

"Lost now, of course, as that sort of magical thingamajig always is. Probably in some secret hiding place in the mosque, or on the finger of some chap who's off living somewhere where there're no birds."

"Or where there are so many," I noted, "that one can't make out what they're saying for the racket. Your story has something of the parable about it, Barclay."

It was at that point that Daniel Thorpe spoke up. He spoke, somehow, impersonally, without looking at us. His English had a peculiar accent, which I attributed to a long stay in the East.

"It is not a parable," he said. "Or if it is, it is nonetheless a true story. There are things that have a price so high they can never be sold."

The words I am attempting to reconstruct impressed me less than the conviction with which Daniel Thorpe spoke them. We thought he was going to say something further, but suddenly he fell mute, as though he regretted having spoken at all. Barclay said good night. Thorpe and I returned together to the hotel. It was quite late by now, but Thorpe suggested we continue our conversation in his room. After a short exchange of trivialities, he said to me:

"Would you like to own King Solomon's ring? I offer it to you. That's a metaphor, of course, but the thing the metaphor stands for is every bit as wondrous as that ring. Shakespeare's memory, from his youngest boyhood days to early April, 1616— I offer it to you."

I could not get a single word out. It was as though I had been offered the ocean.

Thorpe went on:

"I am not an impostor. I am not insane. I beg you to suspend judgment until you hear me out. Major Barclay no doubt told you that I am, or was, a military physician. The story can be told very briefly. It begins in the East, in a field hospital, at dawn. The exact date is not important. An enlisted man named Adam Clay, who had been shot twice, offered me the precious memory almost literally with his last breath. Pain and fever, as you know, make us creative; I accepted his offer without crediting it—and besides, after a battle, nothing seems so very strange. He barely had time to explain the singular conditions of the gift: The one who possesses it must offer it aloud, and the one who is to receive it must accept it the same way. The man who gives it loses it forever."

The name of the soldier and the pathetic scene of the bestowal struck me as "literary" in the worst sense of the word. It all made me a bit leery.

"And you, now, possess Shakespeare's memory?"

"What I possess," Thorpe answered, "are still *two* memories— my own personal memory and the memory of that Shakespeare that I partially am. Or rather, two memories possess *me*. There is a place where they merge, somehow. There is a woman's face . . . I am not sure what century it belongs to."

"And the one that was Shakespeare's——" I asked. "What have you done with it?"

There was silence.

"I have written a fictionalized biography," he then said at last, "which garnered the contempt of critics but won some small commercial success in the United States and the colonies. I believe that's all. . . . I have warned you that my gift is not a sinecure. I am still waiting for your answer."

I sat thinking. Had I not spent a lifetime, colorless yet strange, in pursuit of Shakespeare? Was it not fair that at the end of my labors I find him?

I said, carefully pronouncing each word:

"I accept Shakespeare's memory."

Something happened; there is no doubt of that. But I did not feel it happen.

Perhaps just a slight sense of fatigue, perhaps imaginary.

I clearly recall that Thorpe did tell me:

"The memory has entered your mind, but it must be 'discovered.' It will emerge in dreams or when you are awake, when you turn the pages of a book or turn a corner. Don't be impatient; don't *invent* recollections. Chance in its mysterious workings may help it along, or it may hold it back. As I gradually forget, you will remember. I can't tell you how long the process will take."

We dedicated what remained of the night to a discussion of the character of Shylock. I refrained from trying to discover whether Shakespeare had had personal dealings with Jews. I did not want Thorpe to imagine that I was putting him to some sort of test. I did discover (whether with relief or uneasiness, I cannot say) that his opinions were as academic and conventional as my own.

In spite of that long night without sleep, I hardly slept at all the following night. I found, as I had so many times before, that I was a coward. Out of fear of disappointment, I could not deliver myself up to openhanded hope. I preferred to think that Thorpe's gift was illusory. But hope did, irresistibly, come to prevail. I would possess Shakespeare, and possess him as no one had ever possessed anyone before—not in love, or friendship, or even hatred. I, in some way, would *be* Shakespeare. Not that I would write the tragedies or the intricate sonnets—but I would recall the instant at which the witches (who are also the Fates) had been revealed to me, the other instant at which I had been given the vast lines:

> *And shake the yoke of inauspicious stars*
> *From this world-weary flesh.*

I would remember Anne Hathaway as I remembered that mature woman who taught me the ways of love in an apartment in Lübeck so many years ago. (I tried to recall that woman, but I could only recover the wallpaper, which was yellow, and the light that streamed in through the window. This first failure might have foreshadowed those to come.)

I had hypothesized that the images of that wondrous memory would be primarily visual. Such was not the case. Days later, as I was shaving, I spoke into the mirror a string of words that puzzled me; a colleague informed me that they were from Chaucer's "A. B. C." One afternoon, as I was leaving the British Museum, I began whistling a very simple melody that I had never heard before.

The reader will surely have noted the common thread that links these first revelations of the memory: it was, in spite of the splendor of some metaphors, a good deal more auditory than visual.

De Quincey says that our brain is a palimpsest. Every new text covers the previous one, and is in turn covered by the text that follows—but all-powerful Memory is able to exhume any impression, no matter how momentary it might have been, if given sufficient stimulus. To judge by the will he left, there had been not a single book in Shakespeare's house, not even the Bible, and yet everyone is familiar with the books he so often repaired to: Chaucer, Gower, Spenser, Christopher Marlowe, Holinshed's *Chronicle*, Florio's Montaigne, North's Plutarch. I possessed, at least potentially, the memory that had been Shakespeare's; the reading (which is to say the rereading) of those old volumes would, then, be the stimulus I sought. I also reread the sonnets, which are his work of greatest immediacy. Once in a while I came up with the explication, or with many explications. Good lines demand to be read aloud; after a few days I effortlessly recovered the harsh *r*'s and open vowels of the sixteenth century.

In an article I published in the *Zeitschrift für germanische Philologie*, I wrote that Sonnet 127 referred to the memorable defeat of the Spanish Armada. I had forgotten that Samuel Butler had advanced that same thesis in 1899.

A visit to Stratford-on-Avon was, predictably enough, sterile.

Then came the gradual transformation of my dreams. I was to be granted neither splendid nightmares à la de Quincey nor pious allegorical visions in the manner of his master Jean Paul*; it was unknown rooms and faces that entered my nights. The first face I identified was Chapman's; later there was Ben Jonson's, and the face of one of the poet's neighbors, a person who does not figure in the biographies but whom Shakespeare often saw.

The man who acquires an encyclopedia does not thereby acquire every line, every paragraph, every page, and every illustration; he acquires the *possibility* of becoming familiar with one and another of those things. If that is the case with a concrete, and relatively simple, entity (given, I mean, the alphabetical order of its parts, etc.), then what must happen with a thing which is abstract and variable—*ondoyant et divers?* A dead man's magical memory, for example?

No one may capture in a single instant the fullness of his entire past. That gift was never granted even to Shakespeare, so far as I know, much less to me, who was but his partial heir. A man's memory is not a summation; it is a chaos of vague possibilities. St. Augustine speaks, if I am not mistaken, of the palaces and the caverns of memory. That second metaphor is the more fitting one. It was into those caverns that I descended.

Like our own, Shakespeare's memory included regions, broad regions, of shadow—regions that he willfully rejected. It was not without shock that I remembered how Ben Jonson had made him recite Latin and Greek hexameters, and how his ear—the incomparable ear of Shakespeare—would go astray in many of them, to the hilarity of his fellows.

I knew states of happiness and darkness that transcend common human experience.

Without my realizing it, long and studious solitude had prepared me for the docile reception of the miracle. After some thirty days, the dead man's memory had come to animate me fully. For one curiously happy week, I almost believed myself Shakespeare. His work renewed itself for me. I know that for Shakespeare the moon was less the moon than it was Diana, and less Diana than that dark drawn-out word *moon.* I noted another discovery: Shakespeare's apparent instances of inadvertence— those *absences dans l'infini* of which Hugo apologetically speaks—

were deliberate. Shakespeare tolerated them—or actually interpolated them—so that his discourse, destined for the stage, might appear to be spontaneous, and not overly polished and artificial (*nicht allzu glatt und gekünstelt*). That same goal inspired him to mix his metaphors:

> *my way of life*
> *Is fall'n into the sear, the yellow leaf.*

One morning I perceived a sense of guilt deep within his memory. I did not try to define it; Shakespeare himself has done so for all time. Suffice it to say that the offense had nothing in common with perversion.

I realized that the three faculties of the human soul—memory, understanding, and will—are not some mere Scholastic fiction. Shakespeare's memory was able to reveal to me only the circumstances of *the man* Shakespeare. Clearly, these circumstances do not constitute the uniqueness of *the poet*; what matters is the literature the poet produced with that frail material.

I was naive enough to have contemplated a biography, just as Thorpe had. I soon discovered, however, that that literary genre requires a talent for writing that I do not possess. I do not know how to tell a story. I do not know how to tell *my own* story, which is a great deal more extraordinary than Shakespeare's. Besides, such a book would be pointless. Chance, or fate, dealt Shakespeare those trivial terrible things that all men know; it was his gift to be able to transmute them into fables, into characters that were much more alive than the gray man who dreamed them, into verses which will never be abandoned, into verbal music. What purpose would it serve to unravel that wondrous fabric, besiege and mine the tower, reduce to the modest proportions of a documentary biography or a realistic novel the sound and fury of *Macbeth*?

Goethe, as we all know, is Germany's official religion; the

worship of Shakespeare, which we profess not without nostalgia, is more private. (In England, the official religion is Shakespeare, who is so unlike the English; England's sacred book, however, is the Bible.)

Throughout the first stage of this adventure I felt the joy of being Shakespeare; throughout the last, terror and oppression. At first the waters of the two memories did not mix; in time, the great torrent of Shakespeare threatened to flood my own modest stream—and very nearly did so. I noted with some nervousness that I was gradually forgetting the language of my parents. Since personal identity is based on memory, I feared for my sanity.

My friends would visit me; I was astonished that they could not see that I was in hell.

I began not to understand the everyday world around me (*die alltägliche Umwelt*). One morning I became lost in a welter of great shapes forged in iron, wood, and glass. Shrieks and deafening noises assailed and confused me. It took me some time (it seemed an infinity) to recognize the engines and cars of the Bremen railway station.

As the years pass, every man is forced to bear the growing burden of his memory. I staggered beneath two (which sometimes mingled)—my own and the incommunicable other's.

The wish of all things, Spinoza says, is to continue to be what they are. The stone wishes to be stone, the tiger, tiger—and I wanted to be Hermann Sörgel again.

I have forgotten the date on which I decided to free myself. I hit upon the easiest way: I dialed telephone numbers at random. The voice of a child or a woman would answer; I believed it was my duty to respect their vulnerable estates. At last a man's refined voice answered.

"Do you," I asked, "want Shakespeare's memory? Consider well: it is a solemn thing I offer, as I can attest."

An incredulous voice replied:

"I will take that risk. I accept Shakespeare's memory."

I explained the conditions of the gift. Paradoxically, I felt both a *nostalgie* for the book I should have written, and now never would, and a fear that the guest, the specter, would never abandon me.

I hung up the receiver and repeated, like a wish, these resigned words:

Simply the thing I am shall make me live.

I had invented exercises to awaken the antique memory; I had now to seek others to erase it. One of many was the study of the mythology of William Blake, that rebellious disciple of Swedenborg. I found it to be less complex than merely complicated.

That and other paths were futile; all led me to Shakespeare.

I hit at last upon the only solution that gave hope courage: strict, vast music—Bach.

P.S. (1924)—I am now a man among men. In my waking hours I am Professor Emeritus Hermann Sörgel; I putter about the card catalog and compose erudite trivialities, but at dawn I sometimes know that the person dreaming is that other man. Every so often in the evening I am unsettled by small, fleeting memories that are perhaps authentic.

Afterword by Andrew Hurley

It should hardly be surprising that as Borges, born in 1899, entered his seventies he found it harder to maintain the rhythm of production that he had kept up in his earlier years. In point of fact though, it was no lack of invention or creativity that slowed him down, but rather circumstances. First, perhaps, were the physical obstacles of old age: by now not only was he growing somewhat frail but he was totally blind, and he had to depend on dictation for both his writing and the meticulous revisions that he was famed for. But of course Borges had been dictating for years; what other circumstances were taking their toll? For one thing, he was travelling constantly during the early seventies, both enjoying and hounded by the international fame (in some quarters, almost worship) that had come to him rather belatedly. For another, his mother, Leonor Acevedo, now in her nineties, fell very ill. She had been quite frail for years and had hardly left the house; Borges had been obliged to find companions and caretakers for her, not to mention companions and amanuenses for himself now that his mother could no longer assist him. But then, in 1971, Leonor fell prey to a long, agonizing, and heartwrenching illness; though totally bedridden by 1973, she did not die until 1975, screaming in pain. The security of all that had been "home" and "safe routine" was thus crumbling for Borges in the early seventies. And yet somehow, with all the physical and emotional burdens of this period, Borges still managed to produce three remarkable books of fiction in the last years of his life:

Brodie's Report (published in 1970) and the two included here, *The Book of Sand* (1975) and *Shakespeare's Memory* (1983).

One calls them remarkable, but unfortunately, as is sometimes done with a writer's juvenilia, these late volumes have frequently been treated almost as "geriatrica," dismissed by critics nostalgic for the "good old days" as not up to the high standards of the early work, as exhibiting a lamentable falling-off of imagination—though those critics never, it should be noted, talk about a falling-off of craft. Yet sometimes one wonders whether those commentators are reading the same stories that one is reading, because enough of the stories to tip any critic's scale, one would think—"The Other," "The Night of the Gifts," "The Book of Sand," "Blue Tigers," "Shakespeare's Memory," and probably three more in *Brodie's Report*—are surely as haunting and provocative and well wrought as anything Borges ever wrote.

In fact, one might go even further: if, as those nostalgic critics claim, these are "an old man's stories," one might have the temerity to reply that perhaps they are stories that couldn't have been written by a younger one. For looked at in that way, as stories coming at the end of a rich long life and inescapably arising out of that autumnal time, they have much to say. Foremost, perhaps, one would point to the carefully nuanced motif of loss that runs through the stories. "Ulrikke," "The Disk," and "The Congress" all turn on the loss or squandering of a gift or treasure—love, a fantastic coin of a single side, love and brotherhood in the Congress of Humanity—out of which comes a vast gain in understanding. (In "The Disk," the reader rather than the narrator is the beneficiary of the understanding, but the gain is there, none the less.) Loss in these stories is not negative; as things are lost or fall away, what is left becomes more precious, there is a kind of concentration and distillation that makes what remains all the more bright and glowing. That, too, may be the "moral" that we are to see in the two complementary stories here, "Undr" and "The Mirror and the Mask." Both of these stories deal with the distillation of a poem into a single word, and how striking that is: two stories in one volume dealing with such an odd and specific motif. The inescapable conclusion seems to be that there was something extraordinarily important to Borges there. If one were to pursue one's "old man" theory of these stories, then that loss (or stripping away of all the words of poetry) that is repaid in infinitely greater gain would tell us that as the world turns and a man gains experience, what he learns (if he is lucky or temperamentally well-disposed) is that what counts is the essence, that which lies at the irreducible heart of things. That is, a man comes to see the merely chronological (the merely *syntactical*) as dross, as filler, and when he is able to cast it away he finds that he can live (and compose) all the more richly. He can even die, commit suicide, with joy. And *that* fact, perhaps only an old man—blind, frail, constantly rereading because unable really to read anew, yet still creating tightly-crafted poems that distill a whole life's experience—could tell us. (The other poet's suicide, in "August 25, 1983," is, indeed, portrayed as Borges' own, and "Borges" meets it with calm resignation and relief, one would almost dare say welcome.)

A single distilled word, secret and magical, is also the key to "The Rose of Paracelsus," the story of a weary old alchemist who longs in vain for a disciple fit to receive the wisdom that the old magus has gained from years of alchemical experimentation. This story, like "Undr" and "The Mirror and the Mask," must surely be talking about the purity of the poetics that Borges has at last come to, the poetic ability (equivalent to transforming base stuff into gold) that resides in the most frugal but precise and painstaking employment of one's gifts. Of course it is also about the loneliness of that estate, but when with his single word Paracelsus restores the rose, the sense of triumph, of pride, of achievement, seems ample recompense for the solitude and weariness. Clouds in these last stories do have silvery (or gold) linings.

One might also argue that there is another theme, related to the distillation that comes with stripping-away, that is also pervasive in these stories as it had never been before; that is the notion of memory *as* identity. (Always before, those had been two interlinked but relatively separate themes.) In this twist on the "loss-becomes-gain" motif, that which remains as things fall away—one's memory—is the very essence of the self, for that which remains and glow more brightly, grows more brightly *in memory* and becomes therefore what one most *is*. The reader should not misunderstand; one would not want to make the cliched argument about old age in general—that as one grows old, one begins to live less and less in the external world and more and more in memory. Rather, what we see in a story such as "Shakespeare's Memory" is that it's only when all the outwardness, the accidents and circumstances of life, are stripped away that one begins most fully to discover oneself. It is an argument that is positive, not negative.

In all this, what we sense is that Borges has entered his last years with a gentleness, a sweetness, a tranquility that is enviable. Another man—old, blind, frail, without family (though there were companions)—might become bitter; not so Borges. This is probably clearest in that truly "old man" story, "The Other," in which an elderly Borges meets his younger self. The older man's attitude toward the younger—the slight condescension toward his enthusiasms, the great distance lent by experience, and yet, of course, the tenderness toward the almost-boy that he once was—is, in this regard, most instructive. *How sweet those days were,* Borges seems to be saying, *but how far one has come, and how much one has learned.* The narrator does not miss those youthful enthusiasms, or the "rush" that comes from innovation for innovation's sake; instead, he has learned acceptance, and so he is able to console his younger self, appalled at the older incarnation's sightlessness: "Gradual blindness is not tragic. It's like the slowly growing darkness of a summer evening." The elegiac tone of those words could hardly be so convincingly achieved by a younger writer, and we should not be so knowing (or so cynical) as to disparage it; it is undoubtedly hard won.

In these stories a man can also call upon memory in order to assert not just his personal and particular identity, but also his common humanity. In "The Night of the Gifts," the narrator remembers two "first times"—the first time he made love and the first time he saw a dead man—and recalls, too, how he has spent the rest of his life "sharing" those things with others. These "central" things, as Borges calls them—lovemaking and death—must have been central to Borges indeed, for more than once in his *oeuvre* he quotes that character in Kipling's *Kim* who says, "By fifteen I'd shot my man and begot my man"—as if, says Borges, "the two acts were, essentially, one." Thus, "The Night of the Gifts" tells us that memory can both preserve our sense of identity, of self, and remind us that we are one with others in the "river of history."

And so, with the mention of begetting, we come to the last of what one would take as the "old man" motifs in these volumes— sex. Any reader familiar with Borges is surely bound to notice that these stories ("Ulrikke," "The Congress," and "The Night of the Gifts") have more sex (or "sex") in them than any other stories anywhere in Borges. But of course the sex is accompanied by that haunting line in "Ulrikke"—"For a celibate, middle-aged man, proffered love is a gift that one no longer hopes for"—so that, highly romanticized and haloed, as it were, with nostalgia for what once was (or never was), the sex written into these stories seems to come as the upwelling of a sense of irrecoverable loss, a recognition and admission that one has come to the end of one's corporeal, physical, sensual days. How else to explain the presence of these images just now, at the end of life? Yet once again the irrecoverable loss brings us full circle, to the loss that is a gain— a gain of understanding, of essential humanity, and of a thing to treasure in the memory.

One would be remiss here, speaking of Borges' sweetness,

calm, resignation, his recognition that out of loss comes recompense, and even (dare one say it?) his sublimated carnality, if one did not mention the entry (or re-entry) into his life just at this time of María Kodama, who had been his student and now became his constant companion and then wife through the final fourteen years of his life. Kodama helped Borges deal with fame, the rigors of travel, the complications of writing and publishing, and of course his frailty. Loving, fiercely protective, herself a woman both talented and well-educated (partly by Borges himself), María Kodama unquestionably brought stability, human warmth, protective intimacy, and practical, reliable literary support to Borges' life, and she must be credited with aiding immeasurably in bringing these late fictions about, from inspiration to publication.

Of course these stories have other common leitmotifs—more obvious ones, perhaps, and less "autobiographical," not so connected with the "late life" theory of the stories' composition. They are the same image and genre repetitions that run through Borges' entire career: the double that we meet in "The Other" and "August 25, 1983"; the wandering poet in "The Mirror and the Mask," "Undr," and "A Weary Man's Utopia"; those Borgesian books and libraries in "The Book of Sand," "Shakespeare's Memory," and "The Congress"; magical objects and the irruption of the unexplainable into the world in "The Disk," "The Book of Sand," "Blue Tigers," "The Rose of Paracelsus"; theology and its heresies in "The Sect of the Thirty"; speculations on philosophy and mathematics in the charming story "Blue Tigers"; the history of South America in "Avelino Arrendondo"; a story in the "fantastic" mode in "There Are More Things," which is so similar in its spirit, in the horror caused the narrator by the Other, to the early 'Tlön, Uqbar, Orbis Tertius"; and more of that kind of stories, set far away in time and place and language, that read like parables or myths in "Ulrikke," "The Sect of the Thirty," "The Mirror and the Mask," "Undr," "A Weary Man's Utopia," "The Disk," "The Rose of Paracelsus." In "Avelino Arredondo" we once more find Borges musing, as he had in so many of his most intriguing stories—"The Disinterested Killer Bill Harrigan," "The Shape of the Sword," "The Garden of Forking Paths," "Story of the Warrior and the Captive Maiden," "A Biography of Tadeo Isidoro Cruz," "The Wait," "Emma Zunz," "Averroës' Search," "*Deutsches Requiem*," "The Captive," "Covered Mirrors"—on the absolute otherness of another person's mind and motivations, and in "The Bribe" we find him speculating, much as he did in the more famous story "Guayaquil," on the force of personality in the weaving of human events. The fact is, in the foreword to *Brodie's Report* Borges said it of himself: "A mere handful of arguments have haunted me all these years; I am decidedly monotonous." One has to say that it is a rich monotony, however, one that has been to many readers endlessly fascinating—and now it is enriched even further by the human concerns of loss, resignation, acceptance, and love, and by the author's well-earned celebration of the small triumphs and great power of the word. In the face of this *ave atque vale* so carefully constructed for the reader, cavils over an old man's flagging creativity seem simply another sort of blindness, made visible. These are stories, like all of Borges' stories, that richly repay reading and rereading, and that can be, in their quiet and unassuming way, just as thrilling as the first ones were, all those years ago.

Andrew Hurley
San Juan, Puerto Rico
March 2000

A Note on the Translation

(from Collected Fictions)

The first known English translation of a work of fiction by the
Argentine Jorge Luis Borges appeared in the August 1948 issue
of *Ellery Queen's Mystery Magazine*, but although seven or eight
more translations appeared in "little magazines" and anthologies
during the fifties, and although Borges clearly had his champions
in the literary establishment, it was not until 1962, fourteen years
after that first appearance, that a book-length collection of fiction
appeared in English.

The two volumes of stories that appeared in that *annus mira-
bilis*—one from Grove Press, edited by Anthony Kerrigan, and
the other from New Directions, edited by Donald A. Yates and
James E. Irby—caused an impact that was immediate and overwhelming. John Updike, John Barth, Anthony Burgess, and count-
less other writers and critics have eloquently and emphatically
attested to the unsettling yet liberating effect that Jorge Luis
Borges' work had on their vision of the way literature was
thenceforth to be done. Reading those stories, writers and critics
encountered a disturbingly *other* writer (Borges seemed, sometimes, to come from a place even more distant than Argentina,
another literary planet), transported into their ken by translations,
who took the detective story and turned it into metaphysics,
who took fantasy writing and made it, with its questioning and
reinventing of everyday reality, central to the craft of fiction.
Even as early as 1933, Pierre Drieu La Rochelle, editor of the
influential *Nouvelle Revue Française*, returning to France after

visiting Argentina, is famously reported to have said, "*Borges vaut le voyage*"; now, thirty years later, readers didn't have to make the long, hard (though deliciously exotic) journey into Spanish—Borges had been brought to them, and indeed he soon was being paraded through England and the United States like one of those New World indigenes taken back, captives, by Columbus or Sir Walter Raleigh, to captivate the Old World's imagination.

But while for many readers of these translations Borges was a new writer appearing as though out of nowhere, the truth was that by the time we were reading Borges for the first time in English, he had been writing for forty years or more, long enough to have become a self-conscious, self-possessed, and self-*critical* master of the craft.

The reader of the forewords to the fictions will note that Borges is forever commenting on the style of the stories or the entire volume, preparing the reader for what is to come stylistically as well as thematically. More than once he draws our attention to the "plain style" of the pieces, in contrast to his earlier "baroque." And he is right: Borges' prose style is characterized by a deter- mined economy of resources in which every word is weighted, every word (every mark of punctuation) "tells." It is a quiet style, whose effects are achieved not with bombast or pomp, but rather with a single exploding word or phrase, dropped almost as though offhandedly into a quiet sentence: "He examined his wounds and saw, without astonishment, that they had healed." This laconic detail ("without astonishment"), coming at the very beginning of "The Circular Ruins," will probably only at the end of the story be recalled by the reader, who will, retrospectively and somewhat abashedly, see that it changes *everything* in the story; it is quintes- sential Borges.

Quietness, subtlety, a laconic terseness—these are the marks of Borges' style. It is a style that has often been called intellectual, and indeed it is dense with allusion—to literature, to philosophy, to religion or theology, to myth, to the culture and history of Buenos Aires and Argentina and the Southern Cone of South America, to the other contexts in which his words may have appeared. But it is also a simple style: Borges' sentences are almost invariably classical in their symmetry, in their balance. Borges likes parallelism, chiasmus, subtle repetitions-with-variations; his only indulgence in "shocking" the reader (an effect he repudiated) may be the "Miltonian displacement of adjectives" to which he alludes in his foreword to *The Maker*.

Another clear mark of Borges' prose is its employment of certain words with, or for, their etymological value. Again, this is an adjectival device, and it is perhaps the technique that is most unsettling to the reader. One of the most famous opening lines in Spanish literature is this: *Nadie lo vio desembarcar en la unánime noche*: "No one saw him slip from the boat in the unanimous night." What an odd adjective, "unanimous." It is so odd, in fact, that other translations have not allowed it. But it is just as odd in Spanish, and it clearly responds to Borges' intention, explicitly expressed in such fictions as "The Immortal," to let the Latin root govern the Spanish (and, by extension, English) usage. There is, for instance, a "splendid" woman: Her red hair glows. If the translator strives for similarity of effect in the translation (as I have), then he or she cannot, I think, avoid using this technique— which is a technique that Borges' beloved Emerson and de Quincey and Sir Thomas Browne also used with great virtuosity.

Borges himself was a translator of some note, and in addition to the translations per se that he left to Spanish culture—a number of German lyrics, Faulkner, Woolf, Whitman, Melville, Carlyle, Swedenborg, and others—he left at least three essays on the act of translation itself. Two of these, I have found, are extraordinarily liberating to the translator. In "Versions of Homer" ("Las versiones homéricas," 1932), Borges makes it unmistakably clear that every translation is a "version"—not *the* translation of Homer (or any other author) but *a* translation, one in a never-ending series, at least an infinite *possible* series. The very idea of *the* (definitive) translation is misguided, Borges tells us; there are only drafts, approximations—*versions*, as he insists on calling them. He chides us: "The concept of 'definitive text' is appealed to only by religion, or by weariness." Borges makes the point even more emphatically in his later essay "The Translators of the 1001 Nights" ("Los traductores de las *1001 Noches*," 1935).

If my count is correct, at least seventeen translators have preceded me in translating one or more of the fictions of Jorge Luis Borges. In most translator's notes, the translator would feel obliged to justify his or her new translation of a classic, to tell the potential reader of this new *version* that the shortcomings and errors of those seventeen or so prior translations have been met and conquered, as though they were enemies. Borges has tried in his essays to teach us, however, that we should not translate "against" our predecessors; a new translation is always justified by the new voice given the old work, by the new life in a new land that the translation confers on it, by the "shock of the new" that both old and new readers will experience from this inevitably new (or renewed) work. What Borges teaches is that we should simply commend the translation to the reader, with the hope that the reader will find in it a literary experience that is rich and moving. I have listened to Borges' advice as I have listened to Borges' fictions, and I—like the translators who have preceded me—have rendered Borges in the style that I hear when I listen to him. I think that the reader of my version will hear something of the genius of his storytelling and his style. For those who wish to read Borges as Borges wrote Borges, there is always *le voyage à l'espagnol*.

The text that the Borges estate specified to be used for this new translation is the three-volume *Obras completas*, published by Emecé Editores in 1989.

In producing this translation, it has not been our intention to produce an annotated or scholarly edition of Borges, but rather a "reader's edition." Thus, bibliographical information (which is often confused or terribly complex even in the most reliable of cases) has not been included except in a couple of clear instances, nor have we taken variants into account in any way; the Borges Foundation is reported to be working on a fully annotated, bibliographically reasoned variorum, and scholars of course can go to the several bibliographies and many other references that now exist. I have, however, tried to provide the Anglophone reader with at least a modicum of the general knowledge of the history, literature, and culture of Argentina and the Southern Cone of South America that a Hispanophone reader of the fictions, growing up in that culture, would inevitably have. To that end, asterisks have been inserted into the text of the fictions, tied to corresponding notes at the back of the book. (The notes often cite sources where interested readers can find further information.)

One particularly thorny translation decision that had to be made involved *A Universal History of Iniquity*. This volume is purportedly a series of biographies of reprehensible evildoers, and as biography, the book might be expected to rely greatly upon "sources" of one sort or another—as indeed Borges' "Index of Sources" seems to imply. In his preface to the 1954 reprinting of the volume, however, Borges acknowledges the "fictive" nature of his stories: This is a case, he says, of "changing and distorting (sometimes without æsthetic justification) the stories of other men" to produce a work singularly his own. This sui generis use of sources, most of which were in English, presents the translator with something of a challenge: to translate Borges even while Borges is cribbing from, translating, and "changing and distorting" other writers' stories. The method I have chosen to employ is to go to the sources Borges names, to see the ground upon which those changes and distortions were wrought; where Borges is clearly translating phrases, sentences, or even larger pieces of text, I have used the English of the original source. Thus, the New York gangsters in "Monk Eastman" speak as Asbury quotes them, not as I might have translated Borges' Spanish into English had I been translating in the usual sense of the word; back-translating Borges' translation did not seem to make much sense. But even while returning to the sources, I have made no attempt, either in the text or in my notes, to "correct" Borges; he has changed names (or their spellings), dates, numbers, locations, etc., as his literary vision led him to, but the tracing of those "deviations" is a matter which the editors and I have decided should be left to critics and scholarly publications.

More often than one would imagine, Borges' characters are murderers, knife fighters, throat slitters, liars, evil or casually violent men and women—and of course many of them "live" in a time different from our own. They sometimes use language that is strong, and that today may well be offensive—words denoting membership in ethnic and racial groups, for example. In the Hispanic culture, however, some of these expressions can be, and often are, used as terms of endearment—*negro/negra* and *chino/china* come at once to mind. (I am not claiming that Argentina is free of bigotry; Borges chronicles that, too.) All this is to explain a decision as to my translation of certain terms—specifically *rusito* (literally "little Russian," but with the force of "Jew," "sheeny"), *pardo/parda* (literally "dark mulatto," "black-skinned"), and *gringo* (meaning Italian immigrants: "wops," etc.)—that Borges uses in his fictions. I have chosen to use the word "sheeny" for *rusito* and the word "wop" for *gringo* because in the stories in which these words appear, there is an intention to be offensive—a *character's* intention, not Borges'. I have also chosen to use the word "nigger" for *pardo/parda*. This decision is taken not without considerable soul-searching, but I feel there is historical justification for it. In the May 20, 1996, edition of *The New Yorker* magazine, p. 63, the respected historian and cultural critic Jonathan Raban noted the existence of a nineteenth-century "Nigger Bob's saloon," where, out on the Western frontier, husbands would await the arrival of the train bringing their wives from the East. Thus, when a character in one of Borges' stories says, "I knew I could count on you, old nigger," one can almost hear the slight tenderness, or respect, in the voice, even if, at the same time, one winces. In my view, it is not the translator's place to (as Borges put it) "soften or mitigate" these words. Therefore, I have translated the epithets with the words I believe would have been used in English—in the United States, say—at the time the stories take place.

The footnotes that appear throughout the text of the stories in the *Collected Fictions* are Borges' own, even when they say "Ed."

This translation commemorates the centenary of Borges' birth in 1899; I wish it also to mark the fiftieth anniversary of the first appearance of Borges in English, in 1948. It is to all translators, then, Borges included, that this translation is—unanimously—dedicated.

Andrew Hurley
San Juan, Puerto Rico
June 1998

Acknowledgments

(from Collected Fictions)

I am indebted to the University of Puerto Rico at Río Piedras for a sabbatical leave that enabled me to begin this project. My thanks to the administration, and to the College of Humanities and the Department of English, for their constant support of my work not only on this project but throughout my twenty-odd years at UPR.

The University of Texas at Austin, Department of Spanish and Portuguese, and its director, Madeline Sutherland-Maier, were most gracious in welcoming the stranger among them. The department sponsored me as a Visiting Scholar with access to all the libraries at UT during my three years in Austin, where most of this translation was produced. My sincerest gratitude is also owed those libraries and their staffs, especially the Perry-Castañeda, the Benson Latin American Collection, and the Humanities Research Center (HRC). Most of the staff, I must abashedly confess, were nameless to me, but one person, Cathy Henderson, has been especially important, as the manuscripts for this project have been incorporated into the Translator Archives in the HRC.

For many reasons this project has been more than usually complex. At Viking Penguin, my editors, Kathryn Court and Michael Millman, have been steadfast, stalwart, and (probably more often than they would have liked) inspired in seeing it through. One could not possibly have had more supportive colleagues, or co-conspirators who stuck by one with any greater solidarity.

Many, many people have given me advice, answered questions, and offered support of all kinds—they know who they are, and will forgive me, I know, for not mentioning them all personally; I have been asked to keep these acknowledgments brief. But two people, Carter Wheelock and Margaret Sayers Peden, have contributed in an especially important and intimate way, and my gratitude to them cannot go unexpressed here. Carter Wheelock read word by word through an "early-final" draft of the translation, comparing it against the Spanish for omissions, misperceptions and mistranslations, and errors of fact. This translation is the cleaner and more honest for his efforts. Margaret Sayers Peden (a.k.a. Petch), one of the finest translators from Spanish working in the world today, was engaged by the publisher to be an outside editor for this volume. Petch read through the late stages of the translation, comparing it with the Spanish, suggesting changes that ranged from punctuation to "readings." Translators want to translate, *love* to translate; for a translator at the height of her powers to read a translation in this painstaking way and yet, while suggesting changes and improvements, to respect the other translator's work, his approach, his thought processes and creativity—even to applaud the other translator's (very) occasional strokes of brilliance—is to engage in an act of selflessness that is almost superhuman. She made the usual somewhat tedious editing process a joy.

I would never invoke Carter Wheelock's and Petch Peden's readings of the manuscripts of this translation—or those of Michael Millman and the other readers at Viking Penguin—as giving it any authority or credentials or infallibility beyond its fair deserts, but I must say that those readings have given me a security in this translation that I almost surely would not have felt so strongly without them. I am deeply and humbly indebted.

First, last, always, and in number of words inversely proportional to my gratitude—I thank my wife, Isabel Garayta.

Andrew Hurley
San Juan, Puerto Rico
June 1998

Notes to the Fictions

(from Collected Fictions)

These notes are intended only to supply information that a Latin American (and especially Argentine or Uruguayan) reader would have and that would color or determine his or her reading of the stories. Generally, therefore, the notes cover only Argentine history and culture; I have presumed the reader to possess more or less the range of general or world history or culture that JLB makes constant reference to, or to have access to such reference books and other sources as would supply any need there. There is no intention here to produce an "annotated Borges," but rather only to illuminate certain passages that might remain obscure, or even be misunderstood, without that information.

For these notes, I am deeply indebted to *A Dictionary of Borges* by Evelyn Fishburn and Psiche Hughes (London: Duckworth, 1990). Other dictionaries, encyclopedias, reference books, biographies, and works of criticism have been consulted, but none has been as thorough and immediately useful as the *Dictionary of Borges*. In many places, and especially where I quote Fishburn and Hughes directly, I cite their contribution, but I have often paraphrased them without direct attribution; I would not want anyone to think, however, that I am unaware or unappreciative of the use I have made of them. Any errors are my own responsibility, of course, and should not be taken to reflect on them or their work in any way. Another book that has been invaluable is Emir Rodríguez Monegal's *Jorge Luis Borges: A Literary Biography* (New York: Paragon Press, [paper] 1988), now out of print. In the notes, I have cited this work as "Rodríguez Monegal, p. x."

The names of Arab and Persian figures that appear in the stories are taken, in the case of historical persons, from the English transliterations of Philip K. Hitti in his work *History of the Arabs from the Earliest Times to the Present* (New York: Macmillan, 1951). (JLB himself cites Hitti as an authority in this field.) In the case of fictional characters, the translator has used the system of transliteration implicit in Hitti's historical names in comparison with the same names in Spanish transliteration.— *Translator.*

The Book of Sand

The Other

p. 6: Another Rosas in 1946, much like our kinsman, the first one: The second Rosas, of course, is Juan Domingo Perón, the Fascist military leader who in 1945 was asked to resign all his commissions and retire, and who did so, only (Napoleon-like) to return eight days later to address huge crowds of people and later, in 1946, to be elected president. All this information is from Rodríguez Monegal, who then adds: "he was Argentina's first king" (pp. 390–391). As for "our kinsman," the details are a bit blurry, but Borges seems to have been related, on his father's side, to Rosas. Fishburn and Hughes talk about a "relative of Borges's great-great-grandfather." Borges hated and despised both these men.

p. 9: "Whitman is incapable of falsehood": Daniel Balderston believes that he has identified this poem: "When I heard at the close of the day," in Walt Whitman, *Complete Poetry and Collected Prose,* ed. Justin Kaplan (New York: Library of America), 1982, pp. 276–277. The essay in which Balderston identifies the poem referred to by the older "Borges" is "The 'Fecal Dialectic': Homosexual Panic and the Origin of Writing in Borges," in: *¿Entiendes?: Queer Readings, Hispanic Writing,* ed. Emilie L. Bergmann and Paul Julian Smith (Durham/London: Duke University Press), 1995, pp. 29–45. While these notes are not intended to add "scholarly" information to the text of Borges, this remarkable identification, and the reading that accompanies it, in the translator's view warrants mention. The old man/young man motif, the public/private motif, the issue of "sex in the oeuvre of Borges," readings of a number of important stories, and, to a degree, the issue of violence in the fictions—all of these questions are impacted by Balderston's contentions in this essay.

The Congress

p. 19: The newspaper Ultima Hora*:* The title can be translated in two ways, *The Eleventh Hour* or *The Latest News*, depending on whether one wishes to give it an apocalyptic reading or a quotidian one.

p. 20: Confitería del Gas: This pastry shop (see also the note to p. 48, "Café Aguila," in the story "The Night of the Gifts" in this volume, for a further explanation of this sort of establishment) is located on Alsina between Bolívar and Defensa, about two blocks from the Casa de Gobierno (or as most Porteños know it, the Casa Rosada, or Pink House), at the River Plate end of the avenue that runs from the Casa de Gobierno to the Plaza del Congreso. I have not been able to learn where this café's curious name came from, perhaps a gas-company office in the neighborhood; the problem with translating it into something such as Café Gas is, as the English-language reader will immediately perceive, the hint of indigestion that it (the translation and the name) leaves. Nor is it a truck stop. Clearly, in locating the *confitería* in this neighborhood, JLB is attempting to associate one "congress" with that of the institutionalized government in whose neighborhood it takes up residence. Porteños know this particular *confitería* as more of a pastry shop than a café per se; we are told that the meringues with crème de Chantilly are the house specialty.

p. 22: Rancher from the eastern province: Before Uruguay became a country, in 1828, it was a Spanish colony which, because it lay east of the Uruguay River, was called the Banda Oriental, or "eastern shore." (The Uruguay meets the Paraná to create the huge estuary system called the Río de la Plata, or River Plate; Montevideo is on the eastern bank of this river, Buenos Aires on the west.) "La Banda Oriental" is an old-fashioned name for the country, then, and "*orientales*," or "Easterners," is the equally old-fashioned name for those who live or were born there. Here, the narrator refers to "the eastern province" because for a very long time the shifting status of Uruguay—colony and protectorate of Spain, annex of Brazil and/or Argentina, etc.—led the nationalistic elements in Buenos Aires to consider it an "eastern province" of Argentina. Uruguay was founded on cattle raising.

p. 22: Artigas: José Gervasio Artigas (1764–1850), Uruguayan, a political and military leader who opposed first the Spaniards and then the Argentines who wished to keep the Banda Oriental (the east bank of the River Plate) in fealty to one or another of those powers. When Argentina, instead of supporting the Banda Oriental's independence from Spain, asserted Spain's authority over the area (in part to keep the Brazilians/Portuguese out), Artigas led a huge exodus of citizens out of Montevideo and "into the wilderness." Recognized as a hero in Uruguay, he might not have been so regarded by a cosmopolite such as Glencoe, especially because of his legendary (but perhaps exaggerated) blood-thirstiness and his association with "the provinces" rather than "the city."

p. 23: Wops: "Gringo" was the somewhat pejorative term used for immigrant Italians; the closest English equivalent is "wop." As with all such designations, the tone of voice with which it is spoken will determine the level of offense; it can even be affectionate if spoken appropriately.

p. 24: Calle Junín: At this time, a street lined with brothels, many of which were relatively tame and in which men might not only solicit the services of prostitutes but also have a drink, talk, and generally be "at their ease."

p. 26: Palace of Running Waters: El Palacio de Aguas Corrientes is a building in central Buenos Aires housing a pumping station and some offices for the water company; it is an extravagantly decorated edifice, its walls covered in elaborate mosaic murals—a building that one Porteño described to this translator as "hallucinatory" and "absurd." The official name of this building is the "Grand Gravitational Repository"; it is, according to *Buenos Aires, Ciudad Secreta* by Germinal Nogués (Buenos Aires: Editorial Ruiz Díaz, 2nd ed., pp. 244–245),

located on the block bounded by Avenida Córdoba and calles Riobamba, Viamonte, and Ayacucho. It is set—or at least was—on one of the highest points of the city. The building of the Palace of Running Waters was begun in 1887, and it is a gigantic jigsaw puzzle designed by the Swedish engineer A. B. Nystromer.

All this architectural effort was invested in a building destined to store 72,700,000 liters of water per day, which was the amount estimated to be needed for the daily consumption of the Porteños. . . .

The four walls of this palace . . . were capable of withstanding this pressure without support except at the center of each side. Solid buttresses were also

*incorporated into the design; these were set at intervals between the corner towers
and the central towers, both inside and outside. . . .*

*Vicente Blasco Ibáñez said of this edifice: "This 'palace' is not a palace. It has
arcades and grand doors and windows but it is all a fake. Inside, there are no
rooms. Its four imposing façades mask the retaining walls of the reservoir inside.
The builders tried to beautify it with all this superfluity, so that it would not
offend the aesthetic of the [city's] central streets." [Trans., A.H.]*

p. 27: The chiripá . . . *the wide-legged* bombacha: These are articles
of the dress of the gaucho. The *chiripá* was a triangular worsted shawl
tied about the waist with the third point pulled up between the legs and
looped into the knot to form a rudimentary pant or a sort of diaper. It
was worn over a pair of pantaloons (ordinarily white) that "stick out"
underneath. The *bombacha* is a wide-legged pant that was worn gathered
at the calf or ankle and tucked into the soft boots, sometimes made of
the hide of a young horse, that the gaucho wore. The *bombacha* resembles
the pant of the Zouave infantryman.

p. 27: The mournful characters in Hernández or Rafael Obligado: José
Hernández (1834–1886), author of *Martín Fierro*, a long semi-epic poem
celebrating the gaucho and his life; Rafael Obligado (1851–1920), a
littérateur who hosted a literary salon and founded the Academia Argentina. Obligado was the author of a very well-known poem dealing with
the life of a *payador*, or traveling singer, named Santos Vega. While the
characters in these poems were portrayed not without defects, their lives
and they themselves were to a degree romanticized; as ways of life
per se, the gaucho and the *payador* were part of the mythology of
Argentina. Borges examines these ways of life (and the literature that
chronicled them) in many of his essays.

p. 28: Calle Jujuy near the Plaza del Once: At its northern end Calle
Jujuy runs directly into the Plaza del Once; on the other (north) side of
the Plaza, it has become Puerreydon. Thus, in a sense, it begins at
Rivadavia, where Borges (and apparently all older Porteños) said "the
Southside began." The "Plaza del Once" (pronounced *óhnsay*, not *wunce*)
is generally called "Plaza Once" in Buenos Aires, but the homonymy of
the English and Spanish words makes it advisable, the translator thinks,
to slightly modify the name in order to alert the English reader to the
Spanish ("eleven"), rather than English ("onetime" or "past"), sense of

the word. Plaza Once is one of Buenos Aires' oldest squares, "associated in Borges's memory with horse-drawn carts" (Fishburn and Hughes), though later simply a modern square.

p. 29: Lugones' Lunario sentimental: Leopoldo Lugones (1874–1938) was one of Argentina's most famous and influential (and most talented) poets; the *Lunario sentimental* is a 1909 book of his poetry.

There Are More Things

p. 36: Turdera: A town south of Buenos Aires, rustic and apparently at this time somewhat uninviting (see the story "The Interloper," in the volume *Brodie's Report*, which is set there).

p. 37: Glew: A town near Turdera.

The Night of the Gifts

p. 48: Café Aguila, on Calle Florida near the intersection of Piedad: Here two things need pointing out: First the Café Aguila, whose name in Spanish is the Confitería del Aguila, actually existed. The *confitería* was the equivalent of a coffeehouse or tearoom, a place for conversation and taking one's time over coffee or tea and pastry (or light food) in the late afternoon and early evening. (One might think of Paris.) The Aguila was a center for intellectuals and artists, as this sketch clearly suggests. Second is the location: Calle Florida (pronounced Flor-*ee*-da) was, and remains, at least near the Plaza de Mayo, one of the most exclusive streets in downtown Buenos Aires; this intersection is just one block from that square. Piedad's name was changed to Bartolomé Mitre in 1906; therefore, this story must take place before that date. If this "Borges," like Borges himself, was born in 1899, he must have been just a young boy overhearing this conversation, and the "we," in that case, must be something of a stretch!

p. 51: Juan Moreira: A gaucho turned outlaw (1819–1874) who was famous during his lifetime and legendary after death. Like Jesse James and Billy the Kid in the United States, he was seen as a kind of folk hero, handy with weapons (in Moreira's case a knife), and hunted down and killed (as this story shows) by a corrupt police. That does not mean he was not to be feared by all when he was "on a tear," as this story also shows.

p. 52: Podestá's long hair and black beard: The Podestá family were circus actors. In 1884, some ten years after the outlaw gaucho Juan Moreira's death, Juan de Podestá put on a pantomime version of the life of Moreira. Podestá and the performances were enormously famous, seen by everyone, and surely colored perceptions of the real-life story of Moreira, as movies have colored those of Jesse James and Billy the Kid.

A Weary Man's Utopia

p. 69: Bahía Blanca: A city in Buenos Aires province, south of the city of Buenos Aires; the bay of that name as well. Thus the "future man" has either traveled a bit south or the story itself takes place south of Buenos Aires.

Avelino Arredondo

p. 80: The war that was ravaging the country: This story takes place, as its first sentence reminds us, in 1897, but one must go back some four decades in order to understand the situation. Since the Battle of Monte Caseros in 1852, in which Rosas (whose troops had been occupying Uruguay) had been defeated and with his defeat Uruguay's titular independence had been won, Uruguay had undergone a series of revolts, uprisings, and power struggles that left the country reeling. Constitutional democracy was an experiment that seemed destined to fail. As in Argentina, it was the Whites (Blancos) against the Reds (Colorados), though the parties in Uruguay were conceived somewhat differently from those in Argentina; in some ways, and at the worst of times, they were simply banners under which generals vied for power, and alliances among the generals and among the Southern Cone nations were by nature shifting. Generally speaking, however, the Blancos were the traditional followers of Manuel Oribe; they were conservative, usually Catholic (as opposed to the "freethinkers" JLB sometimes mentions), and tended to favor the rural areas over the cities; thus the party often was led by provincial, landowning caudillos whose gaucho followers made up the largest number of its members. The Colorados were the liberal, urban party, whose roots went back to the nineteenth-century caudillo Fructuoso Rivera; this was the "ruling" party in Uruguay for many years, though one president resigned saying the Uruguayans were an ungovernable people, and though the Whites were constantly

pressuring the Reds (sometimes by armed uprising) for greater representation in the government. Just prior to the time of this story, the
Blancos and Colorados had come to an uneasy truce, and the Cabinet
of Conciliation (*ministerio de conciliación*) was formed. In 1894 the unlikely
(and compromise) Colorado candidate Juan Idiarte Borda was elected
president on the forty-seventh ballot, but in 1897 the uneasy alliance
broke down; Idiarte Borda was perceived as abusing his power, of
engaging in cronyism and neglecting to respect the right of the factions
that elected him to enjoy some of the fruits of power, and perhaps even
of rigging the upcoming elections. Just at this time the Blancos began a
revolt in the interior, led by the gaucho caudillo Aparicio Saravia (see
below). Idiarte Borda apparently perceived this revolt as directed against
himself, but a faction within the Red party perceived it as a power grab
against the entire party, which Idiarte Borda could not really be said to
represent; the prominent national figure José Batlle y Ordoñez gave a
call to arms to this Colorado faction, and suddenly Idiarte Borda found
himself besieged not only by the Blancos but by a large number of his
own party as well. The armed conflicts fought in the interior were
marked by what must seem to us today grisly and cold-blooded brutality
on the part of all contending sides in the skirmishes and battles that
were fought; one history of Uruguay says that by 1897 there was a
general reaction and outcry against the wholesale slitting of the throats
of "prisoners." See, for instance, the story "The Other Duel" in *Brodie's
Report*, which, though not dealing specifically with this conflict, shows
the "naturalness" of this practice to the conflicts of the time.

p. 80: Battle of Cerros Blancos: In the department of Rivera; white
chalk hills, with a creek of the same name at their foot. In 1897 a body
of government troops under General José Villar met insurrectionist
Blanco forces led by Aparicio Saravia; the "battle" (called that, not
"skirmish," because of the ferocity of the fighting rather than the number
of troops) was indecisive, but the Colorados came out marginally ahead.
No prisoners were taken.

p. 80: Aparicio Saravia's gang of gauchos: Saravia (1856–1904) was,
as Fishburn and Hughes tell us, a "landowner and caudillo, uncultured
and politically unsophisticated, whose magnetic personality secured him
a following among the gauchos of the Interior." Saravia and his troops
fought on the Blanco side against the government of Juan Idiarte Borda;

Saravia had long battled for the Blanco cause against the entrenched Colorado governments.

p. 83: [*Traveled*] *through the bay of La Agraciada where the Thirty-three came ashore, to the Hervidero, through ragged mountains, wildernesses, and rivers, through the Cerro he had scaled to the lighthouse, thinking that on the two banks of the River Plate there was not another like it. From the Cerro on the bay he traveled once to the peak on the Uruguayan coat of arms:* La Agraciada is indeed a bay; the Thirty-three were a band of determined patriots under the leadership of Juan Antonio Lavelleja. Lavelleja, a Uruguayan, was the manager of a meat-salting plant in Buenos Aires when the victory at Ayacucho (1824, liberating Peru from the Spaniards) was announced; he was so inspired by patriotic zeal that he gathered his "thirty-three" and they crossed the River Plate to La Agraciada Bay, and several years (and many battles fought by thousands of volunteers) later liberated Uruguay (1828). Hervidero was the place of Artigas' encampment when he ruled the five provinces he had "conquered" and put under Uruguayan rule; this rustic headquarters was on a tableland in the northwest of Uruguay, far from the "capital" city of Montevideo; it showed his "humility" and symbolized his philosophy of government. The Cerro is the conical hill on a spit of land opposite Montevideo; there is a fortress on the top, and a lighthouse, and it is represented in the top right quadrant of the country's coat of arms. All these references are the touchstones of Uruguayan patriotism; Arredondo dreams of his country in its most heroic manifestations.

p. 84: Juan Idiarte Borda: Borda (1844–1897) was the president of Uruguay, elected under the conditions explained in the first note to p. 80, above.

p. 85: The events: The people and events of this story are "true." The real Avelino Arredondo was in fact the assassin of the real Juan Idiarte Borda (1897). An Argentine reader would almost certainly not recognize the name Avelino Arredondo, and a Uruguayan might or might not; that is why there is no note appended to the first appearance of Arredondo's name, in the title, as there is, for example, to the immediately recognizable name of the city of Guayaquil in the story of that name in the volume *Brodie's Report.* But the year, the historical events, the tracing of the legendary "sites" of Uruguayan history, and various other hints at what is about to occur would certainly have given the reader who hailed from the Southern Cone a sense of familiarity; this story would ring a bell. Certainly Borges tried, subtly, though surely, to plant the seeds of that feeling. In his "statement," Arredondo shows that he is of the Batlle faction of the Colorado Party, not the "faction" (made up of cronies) of Idiarte Borda. (See the first note to p. 80, above.)

The Book of Sand

p. 93: The street the library's on: Calle México, the site of the National Library, where Borges was director. The street's name is given in the Spanish-language story as a kind of punch line, but that bang cannot be achieved for the non-Argentine reader by simply naming the street; thus the explicitation.

Shakespeare's Memory

August 25, 1983

p. 100: Adrogué: In the early years of the century, a town south of Buenos Aires (now simply a suburb or enclave of the city) where Borges and his family often spent vacations; a place of great nostalgia for Borges.

The Rose of Paracelsus

p. 117: De Quincey: *Writings,* XIII, 345: "Insolent vaunt of Paracelsus, that he would restore the original rose or violet out of the ashes settling from its combustion—*that* is now rivalled in this modern achievement" ("The Palimpsest of the Human Brain," *Suspiria de Profundis*). The introductory part of de Quincey's essay deals with the way modern chemistry had been able to recover the effaced writing *under* the latest writing on rolls of parchment or vellum, which were difficult to obtain and therefore reused: "The vellum, from having been the setting of the jewel, has risen at length to be the jewel itself; and the burden of thought, from having given the chief value to the vellum, has now become the chief obstacle to its value; nay, has totally extinguished its value." Though this is the thrust of the beginning of de Quincey's argument and seems to inspire "The Rose of Paracelsus," the latter part of the essay turns to memory. This Borges turns to his own uses in

"Shakespeare's Memory," p. 122, perhaps with the idea of unifying the volume of stories thereby. It is perhaps the following lines from de Quincey's essay that inspired the idea in "Shakespeare's Memory": "Chemistry, a witch as potent as the Erictho of Lucan, has exorted by her torments, from the dust and ashes of forgotten centuries, the secrets of a life extinct for the general eye, but still glowing in the embers. . . . What else than a natural and mighty palimpsest is the human brain? . . . Everlasting layers of ideas, images, feelings have fallen upon your brain softly as light. Each succession has seemed to bury all that went before. And yet, in reality, not one has been extinguished." If only we could fan those embers into fire again . . .

Shakespeare's Memory

p. 127: [*De Quincey's*] *master Jean Paul:* Jean Paul Friedrich Richter (1763–1825, pen name Jean Paul) was early influenced by Sterne. While his writings on literary aesthetics influenced Carlyle (who translated him) and many others, it was his dream literature that influenced Novalis and de Quincey.

PENGUIN CLASSICS

www.penguinclassics.com

- Details about every Penguin Classic

- Advanced information about forthcoming titles

- Hundreds of author biographies

- FREE resources including critical essays on the books and their historical background, reader's and teacher's guides.

- Links to other web resources for the Classics

- Discussion area

- Online review copy ordering for academics

- Competitions with prizes, and challenging Classics trivia quizzes

PENGUIN CLASSICS ONLINE

READ MORE IN PENGUIN

In every corner of the world, on every subject under the sun, Penguin represents quality and variety – the very best in publishing today.

For complete information about books available from Penguin – including Puffins, Penguin Classics and Arkana – and how to order them, write to us at the appropriate address below. Please note that for copyright reasons the selection of books varies from country to country.

In the United Kingdom: Please write to *Dept. EP, Penguin Books Ltd, Bath Road, Harmondsworth, West Drayton, Middlesex UB7 0DA*

In the United States: Please write to *Consumer Sales, Penguin Putnam Inc., P.O. Box 12289 Dept. B, Newark, New Jersey 07101-5289.* VISA and MasterCard holders call 1-800-788-6262 to order Penguin titles

In Canada: Please write to *Penguin Books Canada Ltd, 10 Alcorn Avenue, Suite 300, Toronto, Ontario M4V 3B2*

In Australia: Please write to *Penguin Books Australia Ltd, P.O. Box 257, Ringwood, Victoria 3134*

In New Zealand: Please write to *Penguin Books (NZ) Ltd, Private Bag 102902, North Shore Mail Centre, Auckland 10*

In India: Please write to *Penguin Books India Pvt Ltd, 11 Community Centre, Panchsheel Park, New Delhi 110017*

In the Netherlands: Please write to *Penguin Books Netherlands bv, Postbus 3507, NL-1001 AH Amsterdam*

In Germany: Please write to *Penguin Books Deutschland GmbH, Metzlerstrasse 26, 60594 Frankfurt am Main*

In Spain: Please write to *Penguin Books S. A., Bravo Murillo 19, 1° B, 28015 Madrid*

In Italy: Please write to *Penguin Italia s.r.l., Via Benedetto Croce 2, 20094 Corsico, Milano*

In France: Please write to *Penguin France, Le Carré Wilson, 62 rue Benjamin Baillaud, 31500 Toulouse*

In Japan: Please write to *Penguin Books Japan Ltd, Kaneko Building, 2-3-25 Koraku, Bunkyo-Ku, Tokyo 112*

In South Africa: Please write to *Penguin Books South Africa (Pty) Ltd, Private Bag X14, Parkview, 2122 Johannesburg*

READ MORE IN PENGUIN

Published or forthcoming:

Ulysses James Joyce

Written over a seven-year period, from 1914 to 1921, *Ulysses* has survived bowdlerization, legal action and bitter controversy. An undisputed modernist classic, its ceaseless verbal inventiveness and astonishingly wide-ranging allusions confirm its standing as an imperishable monument to the human condition. 'Everybody knows now that *Ulysses* is the greatest novel of the century' Anthony Burgess, *Observer*

Nineteen Eighty-Four George Orwell

Hidden away in the Record Department of the Ministry of Truth, Winston Smith skilfully rewrites the past to suit the needs of the Party. Yet he inwardly rebels against the totalitarian world he lives in, which controls him through the all-seeing eye of Big Brother. 'His final masterpiece ... *Nineteen Eighty-Four* is enthralling' Timothy Garton Ash, *New York Review of Books*

The Day of the Locust *and* The Dream Life of Balso Snell
Nathanael West

These two novellas demonstrate the fragility of the American dream. In *The Day of the Locust*, talented young artist Todd Hackett has been brought to Hollywood to work in a major studio. He discovers a surreal world of tarnished dreams, where violence and hysteria lurk behind the glittering façade. 'The best of the Hollywood novels, a nightmare vision of humanity destroyed by its obsession with film' J. G. Ballard, *Sunday Times*

The Myth of Sisyphus Albert Camus

The Myth of Sisyphus is one of the most profound philosophical statements written this century. It is a discussion of the central idea of absurdity that Camus was to develop in his novel *The Outsider*. Here Camus poses the fundamental question – Is life worth living? – and movingly argues for an acceptance of reality that encompasses revolt, passion and, above all, liberty.

READ MORE IN PENGUIN

Published or forthcoming:

The Diary of a Young Girl Anne Frank

This definitive edition of Anne Frank's diary restores substantial material omitted from the original edition, giving us a deeper insight into her world. 'One of the greatest books of the twentieth century ... If you have never read Anne Frank's diary, or haven't read it for years, this is the edition to buy' *Guardian*

Brideshead Revisited Evelyn Waugh

The most nostalgic of Evelyn Waugh's novels, *Brideshead Revisited* looks back to the golden age before the Second World War. It tells the story of Charles Ryder's infatuation with the Marchmains and the rapidly disappearing world of privilege they inhabit. 'Lush and evocative ... expresses at once the profundity of change and the indomitable endurance of the human spirit' *The Times*

Oranges John McPhee

From Thailand, where the sweetest oranges are as green as emeralds, to Florida oranges so juicy it is said they should be peeled in the bath, the orange exists in bounteous varieties. John McPhee has woven together history, anecdote and science to create a definitive guide to the world of oranges. 'A classic of American reportage. McPhee is quirky, original and intensely curious' Julian Barnes

Wide Sargasso Sea Jean Rhys

Inspired by Charlotte Brontë's *Jane Eyre, Wide Sargasso Sea* is set in the lush landscape of Jamaica in the 1830s. Born into an oppressive colonialist society, Creole heiress Antoinette Cosway meets and marries a young Englishman. But as Antoinette becomes caught between his demands and her own precarious sense of belonging, she is eventually driven towards madness.

READ MORE IN PENGUIN

Published or forthcoming:

Swann's Way Marcel Proust

This first book of Proust's supreme masterpiece, *A la recherche du temps perdu*, recalls the early youth of Charles Swann in the small, provincial backwater of Combray through the eyes of the adult narrator. The story then moves forward to Swann's life as a man of fashion in the glittering world of *belle-époque* Paris. A scathing, often comic dissection of French society, *Swann's Way* is also a story of past moments tantalizingly lost and, finally, triumphantly rediscovered.

Metamorphosis and Other Stories Franz Kafka

A companion volume to *The Great Wall of China and Other Short Works*, these translations bring together the small proportion of Kafka's works that he thought worthy of publication. This volume contains his most famous story, 'Metamorphosis'. All the stories reveal the breadth of Kafka's literary vision and the extraordinary imaginative depth of his thought.

Cancer Ward Aleksandr Solzhenitsyn

One of the great allegorical masterpieces of world literature, *Cancer Ward* is both a deeply compassionate study of people facing terminal illness and a brilliant dissection of the 'cancerous' Soviet police state. Withdrawn from publication in Russia in 1964, it became a work that awoke the conscience of the world. 'Without doubt the greatest Russian novelist of this century' *Sunday Times*

Peter Camenzind Hermann Hesse

In a moment of 'emotion recollected in tranquility' Peter Camenzind recounts the days of his youth: his childhood in a remote mountain village, his abiding love of nature, and the discovery of literature which inspires him to leave the village and become a writer. 'One of the most penetrating accounts of a young man trying to discover the nature of his creative talent' *The Times Literary Supplement*

BY THE SAME AUTHOR

Fictions

Jorge Luis Borges's *Fictions* introduced an entirely new voice into world literature. It is here we find the astonishing accounts of Funes, the man who can forget *nothing*; the French poet who recreated Don Quixote word for word; the fatal lottery in Babylon; the mysterious planet of Tlön; and the library containing every possible book in the whole universe. Here too are the philosophical detective stories and the haunting tales of Irish revolutionaries, gaucho knife fights and dreams within dreams which proved so influential (and yet impossible to imitate). This collection was eventually to bring Borges international fame; over fifty years later, it remains endlessly intriguing.

'One of the most memorable artists of our age' Mario Vargas Llosa

Selected Poems

Universally acclaimed for his dazzling fictions, Jorge Luis Borges always considered himself to be first and foremost a poet. This collection of his poetry, the largest ever to be assembled in English (alongside the original Spanish), includes scores of pieces that have never previously been translated.

Selected from a lifetime's work, the poems explore themes that preoccupied Borges: the enigma of Time and history; the metaphysics of Schopenhauer and Berkeley; the cult of his ancestors and his 'mysterious habit called Buenos Aires'; and the imagery of mirrors, mazes and swords.

'Borges affects me as only the greatest poets can' Clive Wilmer, *Spectator*

BY THE SAME AUTHOR

The Aleph

Although full of philosophical puzzles and supernatural surprises, the stories which make up *The Aleph* also contain some of Borges's most fully realized human characters. With uncanny insight he takes us inside the minds of an unrepentant Nazi, an imprisoned Mayan priest, fanatical Christian theologians, a woman plotting vengeance on her father's 'killer' and a man awaiting his assassin in a Buenos Aires guest house. This volume also contains the hauntingly brief vignettes about literary imagination and personal identity, collected in *The Maker*, which Borges created as failing eyesight and public fame began to undermine his sense of self.

'He has lifted fiction away from the flat earth where most of our novels and short stories still take place' John Updike

Labyrinths

Jorge Luis Borges was a literary spellbinder whose gripping tales of magic, mystery and murder are shot through with deep philosophical paradoxes. This collection brings together many of his stories, including the celebrated 'Library of Babel', 'Garden of Forking Paths', 'Funes the Memorious' and 'Pierre Menard, Author of the Quixote'.

In later life, dogged by increasing blindness, Borges used essays and brief tantalizing parables to explore the enigmas of time, identity and imagination. Playful and disturbing, scholarly and seductive, his is a haunting and utterly distinctive voice.

'Probably the greatest 20th century author never to win the Nobel prize' *Economist*

BY THE SAME AUTHOR

Brodie's Report

At the age of seventy, after a gap of twenty years, Jorge Luis Borges returned to writing short stories. In *Brodie's Report* and *In Praise of Darkness* he returned also to the style of his earlier years with its brutal realism, its nightmares and its bloodshed. Many of these stories, such as 'Unworthy' and 'The Other Duel', are set in the macho Argentinian underworld, although even the rivalries between academics or artists, as in 'The Duel', are shot through with suppressed violence. Yet many other themes – fate and freewill, friendship and loyalty, time and memory – are threaded through these compelling stories, which are among the finest Borges ever wrote.

'One of the most original and inventive writers of any century' *New Statesman*

The Total Library   Non-Fiction 1922–1986

Though celebrated in the English-speaking world for his poetry and fiction, Borges is equally revered in Latin America for his non-fiction. Now more than 150 of his most brilliant pieces, many of which have never appeared in English before, are brought together for the first time. Learned, lively and endlessly curious, this sparkling collection sees Borges move effortlessly between subjects as diverse as Schopenhauer, angels, Alfred Hitchcock, Oscar Wilde, King Kong, Buddhism, Nazi propaganda and the History of the Tango, and includes his acclaimed essays on Dante.

'A remarkable collection ... witty and elaborate, in turn intimate and magisterial ... his is the literature of eternity' Peter Ackroyd, *The Times*

Published or forthcoming:

The Book of Imaginary Beings
A Universal History of Iniquity